Grace

But that would change, she told herself. Thank God, she no longer loved Denton. Her fixation on him was about loneliness and lust. But that was a disastrous combination. Her heart knew they had no future—that he merely wanted to make love to her, then walk away like before.

They were from two different worlds, and that wasn't going to change. Nor did she want it to. She couldn't survive in the city, and he couldn't survive in the country. But their differences went much deeper than locale.

She had known the boy. She didn't know the man.

Would she get the chance…?

Dear Reader,

Welcome to Silhouette Desire, where you can indulge yourself every month with six passionate, powerful and provocative romances! And you can take romance one step further.... Look inside for details about our exciting new contest, "Silhouette Makes You a Star."

Popular author Mary Lynn Baxter returns to Desire with our MAN OF THE MONTH when *The Millionaire Comes Home* to Texas to reunite with the woman he could never forget. Rising star Sheri WhiteFeather's latest story features a *Comanche Vow* that leads to a marriage of convenience...until passionate love transforms it into the real thing.

It's our pleasure to present you with a new miniseries entitled 20 AMBER COURT, featuring four twentysomething female friends who share an address...and their discoveries about life and love. Don't miss the launch title, *When Jayne Met Erik,* by beloved author Elizabeth Bevarly. The scandalous Desire miniseries FORTUNES OF TEXAS: THE LOST HEIRS continues with *Fortune's Secret Daughter* by Barbara McCauley. Alexandra Sellers offers you another sumptuous story in her miniseries SONS OF THE DESERT: THE SULTANS, *Sleeping with the Sultan.* And the talented Cindy Gerard brings you a touching love story about a man of honor pledged to marry an innocent young woman with a secret, in *The Bridal Arrangement.*

Treat yourself to all six of these tantalizing tales from Silhouette Desire.

Enjoy!

Joan Marlow Golan

Joan Marlow Golan
Senior Editor, Silhouette Desire

Please address questions and book requests to:
Silhouette Reader Service
U.S.: 3010 Walden Ave., P.O. Box 1325, Buffalo, NY 14269
Canadian: P.O. Box 609, Fort Erie, Ont. L2A 5X3

The Millionaire Comes Home

MARY LYNN BAXTER

™ Silhouette®

Desire®

Published by Silhouette Books

America's Publisher of Contemporary Romance

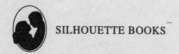 SILHOUETTE BOOKS

ISBN 0-373-76387-5

THE MILLIONAIRE COMES HOME

Copyright © 2001 by Mary Lynn Baxter

This edition published by arrangement with Harlequin Books S.A.

® and TM are trademarks of Harlequin Books S.A., used under license.
Trademarks indicated with ® are registered in the United States Patent
and Trademark Office, the Canadian Trade Marks Office and in other
countries.

Visit Silhouette at www.eHarlequin.com

Printed in U.S.A.

Books by Mary Lynn Baxter

Silhouette Desire

Shared Moments #24
Added Delight #527
Winter Heat #542
Slow Burn #571
Tall in the Saddle #660
Marriage, Diamond Style #679
And Baby Makes Perfect #727
Mike's Baby #781
Dancler's Woman #822
Saddle Up #991
Tight-Fittin' Jeans #1057
Slow-Talkin' Texan #1177
Heart of Texas #1246
Her Perfect Man #1328
The Millionaire Comes Home #1387

Silhouette Special Edition

All Our Tomorrows #9
Tears of Yesterday #31
Autumn Awakening #96
Between the Raindrops #360

Silhouette Intimate Moments

Another Kind of Love #19
Memories that Linger #52
Everything But Time #74
A Handful of Heaven #117
Price Above Rubies #130
When We Touch #156
Fool's Music #197
Moonbeams Aplenty #217
Knight Sparks #272
Wish Giver #296

Silhouette Books

A Day in April

Silhouette Christmas Stories 1992
"Joni's Magic"

36 Hours
Lightning Strikes

MARY LYNN BAXTER

A native Texan, Mary Lynn Baxter knew instinctively that books would occupy an important part of her life. Always an avid reader, she became a school librarian, then a bookstore owner, before writing her first novel.

Now Mary Lynn Baxter is an award-winning author who has written more than thirty novels, many of which have appeared on the *USA Today* list.

One

He wondered if she still lived here.

Denton Hardesty scoffed at his thoughts of his old girlfriend as he braked his BMW at the first and only stoplight in Ruby, Texas. He couldn't believe he'd been born in this one-horse town and lived here until he'd left for college. But Ruby had been his parents' home; he'd had no choice.

Thank heavens he had a choice now. Dallas, the city *he* called home, was a far cry from this quaint little tourist town with its bed-and-breakfast lodgings, antique and gift shops. Too quiet to suit him. As soon as he finished his meeting with his prospective client, regardless of whether a deal was cemented, he would hit the road again, back to Big D.

When he heard a truck honk from behind Denton realized he'd been camped at the light. Muttering under his breath, he shoved down on the accelerator only to have the engine sputter, then quit completely.

A few choice words escaped his lips as he watched the truck swerve around him, a killer look on the driver's face. So, all of Ruby wasn't that laid-back. With dark amusement, Denton found that somewhat comforting as he restarted the BMW. It died on him again directly in front of a service station, the old-fashioned kind where a sign said owner/ mechanic on duty—only in Small Town, USA.

The owner came out immediately, wiping his greasy hands on an equally greasy rag. He smiled, showing off crooked teeth stained with tobacco. "Howdy, need some help?"

Denton figured that went without saying but refrained from stating the obvious, keeping his impatience on a short leash. "My engine's giving me trouble. Mind if I leave it here until the dealership can come get it?"

"Don't mind atall, only how 'bout I take a look at it?"

Denton eyed the tall, lanky man with suspicion. "You know something about foreign cars?"

"Use to work on 'em, especially these." The man nodded toward the sleek black vehicle.

Somehow Denton believed him, even though it seemed unlikely anyone who knew how to work on BMWs would be stuck running a one-man station. But stranger things had happened, he reminded himself ruefully.

"Maybe it's just something minor, and I can have you on your way real soon," the attendant pointed out. "If not, you can call the dealer and nothing will be lost."

Except my valuable time, Denton thought, irritated beyond measure. Curbing his impatience, he made a gesture and said, "Be my guest. See what you can do."

"By the way, my name's Raymond."

"Denton Hardesty."

Raymond stuck out his grimy hand. Then, as if seeing the look on Denton's face, jerked it back and gave a sheepish smile. "Sorry, it's still a bit greasy."

"No problem," Denton muttered, clearly distracted.

"You just passing through?" Raymond asked, his head cocked to one side.

Denton wasn't about to indulge in small talk, not when he had much bigger fish to fry. Besides, for a spring day it was hotter than hell, and he didn't want to be wet with sweat when he met with his client. "Yeah, you might say that."

For once Raymond didn't comment.

"Is there someplace cool where I can get a cup of coffee while I wait?" Denton asked.

Raymond nodded toward a bed-and-breakfast. "Across the street."

"Thanks," Denton said, turning and heading in that direction. The first thing about the two-story colonial style mansion that caught his attention was the lovely grounds: manicured lawns, landscaped flower beds, lilacs and big oak trees, and annual beds that flanked the walkway and proudly lined the front of the porch.

The colors of the mixed annuals were so vivid they were almost blinding. Even though he hadn't set foot on the property, he could smell the lilacs. They offered their ethereal scent and exquisite blossoms to all the passersby. Lucky souls, he thought, remembering the lilacs in his own front yard when he was a youngster.

As he approached the sidewalk, his gaze settled on the porch. Country calm, he reminded himself, a gentle breeze acting as a coolant to his damp skin. Great if you could stand it…. He could tolerate this setting maybe a day, two max, then he'd be climbing the walls. He preferred the sound of horns and car doors slamming. Also, it was imperative he hear the sound of human voices as opposed to the chirp of birds.

Yet, he might have felt differently if he and Grace had…

Ah, to hell with those thoughts. While his memories of living here were for the most part good, Denton couldn't imagine ever doing so again under any circumstances.

When his dad had been transferred out of state the summer of his junior year in college, he hadn't been happy. He'd admit that. He hadn't wanted to leave Grace even though what had happened between them had scared the hell out of him. However, his parents were not about to leave him behind. Once they moved, the unthinkable had happened. His dad had fallen victim to a stroke, something else that had torn him in two.

Suddenly forcing his mind off that dark period and back on more pleasant thoughts, Denton's gaze swept his surroundings. Up close he could see the house needed some repairs, especially the porch, though the state of disrepair didn't dilute any of its charm. What a perfect place for guests to gather for nonsensical conversation and summer breezes.

A wicker swing and settee, along with several

creaky rockers, provided a Norman Rockwell type setting familiar to porches across the South. The only things missing from the ideal picture were platters of watermelon and pitchers of lemonade that would provide wholesome refreshments for the guests. It was a safe bet both would most likely appear later on in the day.

Thinking of lemonade made him thirsty. But the thought didn't last long, knowing what he really needed was another stiff cup of coffee which never failed to give him the extra push he needed to get through his hectic days and nights. He still had a long way to go before this day was over. And the way it had started out didn't bode well.

Maybe the owner would be obliging this late, sunny morning and provide him with that much-needed kick. After slapping at a bee buzzing around his head, Denton lifted the old-fashioned door knocker and let it go.

Grace Simmons hummed to herself as she finished putting away the last of the clean breakfast dishes. She paused in her actions and peered out the back window at the grounds of Grace House. As always, her breath instantly caught and held.

Tulips, her favorite sign of spring, blended together to form a tapestry of natural beauty nothing could ever surpass.

Hers.

This was all hers. And the bank's, she corrected mentally. But such wouldn't always be the case, she reaffirmed with conviction. One day she'd get it paid off, then she'd be the proud owner of this graceful old house. She'd bought it for a song, but in order to make it habitable, then fulfill her dream of turning it into a profitable bed-and-breakfast, she'd had to borrow an additional healthy sum of money.

Still, she paid her banker each month with a cheerful heart, knowing what she wanted to do would work and eventually pay its own way. And while the profit margin remained ever so slim, she was able to keep herself and the home afloat and pay the bank. For the time being that was all that was important.

Extra money for more repairs to the old home would come. She didn't know when or from what source, but she wasn't worried about it. In fact, she didn't worry period. Not anymore. She had learned long ago what worrying did to her, and she could no longer allow herself that indulgence, especially since she ran a business in which other people depended on her.

And she thrived on the never-ending challenge of providing her guests with the cleanest rooms, the loveliest ambiance and the best breakfast she could, at an affordable cost.

As a result her house stayed at full occupancy year-round. However, at present she had one room not booked—a rare occurrence. Yet she wasn't concerned. The right person would show up, and the room would be waiting.

A smile brightened Grace's face as her eyes fastened on a bluebird perched on a limb, grooming himself. Spying on a wild creature was such a small thing, but she had learned, the hard way, it was the small things that made life worth living.

So what if she was a woman alone in a couples' world? So what if she was often lonely, especially in her big bed at night? So what if she wished for what was apparently not going to happen—a happy marriage and children?

So what?

After all she'd been through, she could accept that and be glad for the peace and tranquility that now shaped and dominated her life. Besides, her life was too full to dwell on past mistakes and future longings. At thirty-two she had wasted enough time on something that had brought her heartache rather than joy. At present she was only concentrating on the joy.

Living and working in Ruby, Texas, did just that.

Thinking of work made Grace realize she had too much to do to stand and gaze outdoors, even if it was candy for the soul. She would put her grounds up against anyone else's in town, though she could only take credit for the flowers. Those she did plant and maintain, a full-time job in itself. Because of her part-time helper, Connie Foley, Grace was able to create her miracles outdoors, which she knew brought pleasure to her guests.

Maybe later she would cut some of the tulips for the sunroom, definitely before afternoon snack time, a fun ritual that only two of her present occupants would take advantage of—the elderly couple who were honeymooning. A wider smile forced her dimple deeper in her right cheek as she thought about Ed and Zelma Brenner. In their seventies, and giddily in love, they were a hoot. After both had married someone else, borne children, then widowed, they met on a cruise and married five days later.

On their way to a planned honeymoon at a cottage on Lake Austin, the couple had driven through Ruby. They never made it any farther. According to Ed, the minute they saw Grace House, they had been enchanted and chose to stay there. Hence, Grace had been honored with their presence for over two weeks now. Each day she grew more fond of them. If her parents hadn't died in a freak auto accident when she was in college, she wondered if they would have turned out like Ed and Zelma. She liked to think so, since the thought was somehow comforting.

Her other guest, however, was cut from a far different bolt of cloth. Ralph Kennedy was a well-known children's author who sought complete solitude for the purpose of penning his stories. Here he had apparently found his niche because he'd been a guest for more than four weeks. His brief appearance at breakfast was about all she ever saw of him except on rare occasions when she'd catch him strolling through the grounds. She suspected he was trying to work through a story problem. Despite the fact that he wasn't her usual outgoing boarder, rather weird to be exact, she had no complaints. He paid his weekly bill and seemed content. That was all that mattered.

Deciding it was time to get back to her chores, Grace grabbed a dust cloth out of the cabinet. Opting to keep on her apron, which she loved to wear in spite of its being out of vogue, she made her way out of the large, bright kitchen and headed toward the garden room. It was her favorite room in the entire house, a hard choice to make as the rest of the old dwelling had other bragging rights. The polished hardwood floors, which made no attempt to soak up the sounds of hard-soled shoes, were magnificent. Another favorite was the exquisitely gorgeous Waterford chandelier that hung in the foyer.

She gave a cursory glance to the arched doorways and beveled glass of the front door, to the antique

furnishings as she went into the garden room that was
a prime environment for lush plants. Grace had seen
to it that the room was much more than that since the
living room flowed into it, providing an informal but
lush setting in which to relax over breakfast with a
newspaper or good book or to sip afternoon tea.

Grace had wanted the room to seem drenched in
light. So she had painted the walls a pearly white,
keeping the furniture to a minimum and dispensing
with drapes altogether. She had achieved her goal, the
space becoming a charming blend of yellows and
greens, mixed with seasoned wicker, plump cushions
and pillows and a myriad of flowering bushes and
plants.

On one wall she'd painted an ivy-covered trellis.
Even in the dead of winter the garden room gave one
the feeling of being constantly bathed in greenery and
light.

She had just begun dusting the glass-topped coffee
table when the doorbell chimed. Stuffing her cloth
into her apron pocket, she hurried to open the door,
only to cling to the doorknob for support.

Grace would have recognized him anywhere, regardless of the fourteen years since she'd seen him.
Denton Hardesty, a ghost from the past.

It was obvious from the stunned look on his face
that he hadn't expected to see her, either, as his mouth
was slightly open while his green eyes narrowed.

"Grace," he finally muttered, his tone hoarse as if
he had a sore throat.

"Hello, Denton," she responded, staring at the
man who, one starlit night, took her virginity and her
heart with him.

Two

Somehow Grace managed to derail that traumatic thought and force herself to behave as though Denton Hardesty were a stranger, someone she'd never known. But that wasn't easy, as she was more than a little overwhelmed and flustered by his showing up on her doorstep out of the blue. Holding on to her fractured composure was even more difficult because her senses had leaped at the sight of him.

Dear Lord, that would never do.

"What on earth are you doing here?" she finally asked, the silence having built to an almost thundering roar, at least to her. Maybe it was the sound of her heart beating. Absurd. She no longer gave a fig about him.

"I could ask you the same thing."

"I live here," she said simply, feeling her chin jut slightly and her spine stiffen.

As if he picked up on the slight edge of defiance in her posture, he sighed. "I was wondering if you'd ever left."

"Again, what brings you back to Ruby?"

His sigh deepened. "So that's the way it's going to be?"

For a second Grace was confused. "Excuse me?"

"I can't say that I blame you for not inviting me in."

Grace flushed, realizing that she hadn't budged so much as an inch since she'd opened the door. In fact, she seemed to be guarding the door as if he was an intruder who might force himself inside. In a way that was exactly what he was. However, she had no intention of letting him know that her senses still hadn't quite settled, that his unexpected presence had definitely thrown her for a curve.

"Of course you may come in."

His head leaned to one side. "Are you sure?"

"Certainly," she said, swallowing her irritation at his assumption that she gave a damn one way or the other. She'd best be careful. He'd always had the uncanny ability to read her heart. But that was then, when she was just a teenager. Now she was an adult and he didn't know beans about her.

Finally she stepped back and gestured with one hand. "Welcome to Grace House."

He pulled up short. "You mean this is your place?"

"Yes." Again her tone held a note of defiance, this time with an edge of acid.

Denton chuckled. "I see you haven't lost that sharp tongue."

"Some things never change," she said, more breathlessly than she intended.

"In some cases that's not bad."

It wasn't so much what he said as the way he said it that set off a warning inside her. That raspy note in his voice was just as much a turn-on now as back then. What had she done to deserve this cruel twist of fate? She'd never expected to lay eyes on her first love again.

And why now, when she was lonelier than she'd ever been?

"I'm impressed."

Grace forced herself back to the moment, though what she really wanted to do was tell him to leave, to go back where he came from and not disrupt her life one more second.

Instead she made her way into the garden room and watched as he strode to the long expanse of windows before turning and facing her again.

"Would you like a glass of iced tea?" she asked. "Or would you rather have coffee?"

"Both, actually."

A spontaneous laugh erupted before she could control it. "That's not a problem."

He answered with a smile that hit her like a sledgehammer. He was still too good-looking for words, even if the added grooves of maturity made him appear older than his thirty-four years, two years her senior.

Too, there was an uptightness, a restlessness that she didn't remember. But it had been so long since that summer evening after her last year in high school, when she'd been so madly in love with him, she couldn't be expected to remember every detail about him. Nor did she want to.

Liar.

Right now she was standing there like an idiot, soaking up every detail about him. His hair, while still brown, was now dusted with silver. Not a bad thing, she noted, since the silver highlighted his tanned skin and green eyes that were surrounded by such thick lashes they appeared darker and sootier than they actually were.

As for his over-six-foot frame, he hadn't added an ounce of fat to it. At one time he'd had washboard abs, and since his knit shirt hugged him in all the right places, she knew that hadn't changed. Nor had his long legs and powerful thighs. When her gaze reached that part of his anatomy, and she saw the slight bulge behind his zipper, she averted her eyes back to his face. Those perfect white teeth hadn't changed, either. Or that smile. Both had always been high-wattage and still were.

Not fair.

Here she was, aging, gathering wrinkles in all the wrong places. So what? It didn't matter whether the years had been kind to her or not. Except that it did. Granted, Denton was just passing through, but it was important to her that she at least didn't look like the wrath of God, for heaven's sake.

Then it hit her she was still wearing her apron.

Feeling her cheeks flood with color, she reached for the sash at the back and jerked it.

"Don't."

Her head jolted up. "Don't what?"

"Take it off."

Her hands stilled, and when she opened her mouth to speak, nothing came out.

"It's...different."

Grace rolled her eyes. "Right."

"No, I'm serious."

"What you are is 'seriously' making fun."

"Somehow it suits you."

"You don't have a clue what suits me," Grace snapped, then mentally kicked herself.

"True," he said, his mouth slightly downturned. "But I know what I like, and I like your apron."

"Fine. But I don't." She jerked it off and headed toward the kitchen. "I'll get the drinks and be right back."

"Need any help?" he called to her back.

She didn't so much as slow down. "No, thanks."

By the time she had a tray filled with both iced tea and coffee, her hands were shaking. It was a miracle she had glasswear of any kind left. Just get through this, she told herself. Be polite, make small talk, then get rid of him. Send him back from whence he came.

Blowing out a deep breath, Grace planted a smile on her face and went back into the garden room. Denton had taken a seat in one of the wicker chairs. When he saw her, however, he rose and reached for the tray.

She shook her head, then set it down on the coffee table in front of the settee. "Your choice?"

"Coffee," he said, reaching for it on his own.

She chose a glass of iced tea. For a moment they each sipped in silence, though for Grace that silence still had undertones of booming thunder.

"This is really yours?"

"You sound like that's not possible."

"Hey, that's not it at all. It's just that I'm impressed."

"Impressed, huh?"

"Yeah, impressed. This is a grand old house, and apparently you've made a success of operating it as a bed-and-breakfast. To me that's impressive."

"I'd like to think so. I know that I love every minute of being an innkeeper, so to speak."

"You would. It fits your personality to a T."

Again she wanted to tell him he didn't know jack about her personality, but she refrained. She was already in water over her head. Why purposely drown herself?

"Did you buy the old place?"

"I'm buying it. Right now the bank and I are partners."

He chuckled. "I hear you."

"One of these days, though, it'll be mine free and clear."

"You're that busy?"

"Ruby's grown, despite the fact that it maintains its status as a quiet country town. Being so close to Austin has given us the tourist boost we needed to grow our economy."

"I noticed several antique stores as I drove down main street. Ruby never had anything like that before."

"Again, it's the boom going on in Austin that's responsible."

He looked around for a moment, then faced her again, his eyes probing. If only he didn't have that certain way of staring at a woman as if she was the only person on the face of the earth. Denton could rival Richard Gere when it came to that feat. At one time she'd loved that. Now she hated it.

"You look great, Grace. Have I told you that?"

A warmth spread through her, which she promptly ignored. "No, but that's okay. I'd rather talk about you."

"I'm sure you're curious."

"Let's just say I know you're not passing through for old time's sake."

Did he flush or had she imagined that?

"You're right," he said, reaching for his coffee and taking a drink. "I'm here to see a client."

"In Ruby?" She didn't bother to mask her astonishment.

"A quirk of fate. What can I say?"

"Whatever," she said, hearing that breathlessness in her tone again and wishing she could get her act together.

He set his cup down, then crossed an ankle over the other knee. "I'm an investment broker in Dallas, have been for several years now."

"That's nice."

He chuckled. "'How boring' is what you're really saying."

"I wish you'd stop trying to second-guess me," she said, trying to control her edginess but failing miserably.

"I was always pretty good at doing that, if you'll remember."

His voice had dropped to a husky pitch, and his eyes were so intent on her lips that she felt a rush of color to her face while all the air seemed to have been sucked out of the room. "Look—"

"Sorry. I didn't mean to go down that road. It's

just that I never expected to see you again, especially not here in Ruby.''

''Just because you hauled it—''

His lips thinned. ''You're right to be pissed.''

''Look, Denton, I'm not pissed, okay? Let's just leave the past where it is. Buried.''

''So my car just broke down. How's that for a mundane topic of conversation?''

Ignoring his hint of sarcasm, she asked, ''Where?''

''At the station across the street.'' Denton went on to explain what was going on.

''Ah, Raymond's in charge.'' Her lips quirked in a smile. ''No doubt he's proudly displaying that BMW for all the town to see.''

''Reckon?''

They both laughed at Denton's choice of words. Then, realizing how chummy that sounded, Grace sobered. ''What if he can't fix it?''

''The dealership in Austin will have a loaner car here in no time.''

My, my, how nice, she almost said in a snippy tone, but didn't. Obviously, he was making money hand over fist. She wondered which rancher in Ruby had the kind of big dollars it would take to invest with him? She wasn't about to ask, for several reasons, the main one being she wanted to get rid of him. The longer this indulgence stretched itself, the more dangerous it became to her peace of mind, especially with his gaze seemingly fixed on her breasts.

In spite of her efforts to the contrary, the color lingered in her face. ''You're welcome to wait here,'' she said, glancing away.

''Are you sure?''

His husky tone drew her back. "I even have a vacant room," she quipped.

"I just might take you up on that."

Her jaw went slack. "I didn't—"

"I know you didn't mean it, but I do."

"We both know that's not going to happen."

Both of his eyebrows shot up. "I wouldn't bet on it."

"Are you married?" she asked bluntly, more for herself than for him. She was desperate to steer things back on course after she'd opened her mouth again when she shouldn't have. But no way was he going to remain in Ruby. The thought of him sleeping in her place as a guest was ludicrous and she wouldn't let it happen.

"Not anymore," he said in answer to her question.

"Ah, so there was a Mrs. Denton Hardesty?"

"*Was* is the correct word."

"Not an amiable parting, huh?"

"Not hardly."

"Sorry."

"Me, too. I hate failing at anything. But nothing about our relationship was right from the beginning. Thank goodness there were no children."

She wanted to amen that but didn't.

"What about you? I don't see a ring on your finger."

"There hasn't been one."

He raised his eyebrows again. "I find that hard to believe."

"That I'm an old maid?"

Denton made a snorting sound as his gaze roamed hotly and blatantly over her. "You know better than that."

She turned away, her heart in her throat, feeling the inability to handle much more of this togetherness. "Let's just say I'm happy with my life the way it is."

"There's nothing wrong with that."

A silence fell between them during which she made a conscious effort not to meet his eyes.

It was then his cell phone rang. Grace tried to ignore what he was saying by concentrating on what she was going to serve for snack time. The Brenners would be back shortly, and on rare occasions even Ralph was known to appear for the afternoon goodies.

Only after Denton shoved his cell back into its clip did she face him again.

"I've been stood up, at least for today."

"Oh?"

"My client had an unexpected emergency to deal with. That was his housekeeper."

Relief almost made her giddy. "I guess you'll have to come back to Ruby another time."

Their eyes met and held for the longest time.

"I have a better idea. I'll take that vacant room and hang around."

Three

———

Panic paralyzed her.

Stay. He didn't mean that, not for a minute. He was just jerking her chain again. That had to be the case. It just had to. She almost laughed at the very idea.

In an unsteady tone, she voiced her thoughts. "You're really joking."

His eyes took on a warm, lazy cast as they swept over her. "Is that your way of saying I'm not welcome?"

She swallowed, quelling the urge to slug him. He was baiting her, and she didn't have a clue why. After all, he'd been the one who'd walked out on her. If anyone had an ax to grind, it was she.

"Of course, you're welcome. It's just that—"

"It's just what?" he pressed.

"I can't imagine why you'd want to stay here." There, she'd said it. She'd been as blunt as she knew how to be. If that didn't do the trick then nothing would.

"Can't you?"

Denton's tone suddenly matched his eyes, adding to her confusion. Was he flirting with her? Suddenly the feelings of acute sexual awareness that hung between them was overridden by a sense of outrage. How dare he think he could just show up on her doorstep and behave in such a brazen manner? She had to call a halt to such madness right now. She wasn't about to let him back inside her life only to have him walk out again.

"No, I can't," she said through tight lips. "You don't belong here anymore."

A flash of anger darkened his eyes. Yet, when he spoke his tone was even. "Is a room available?"

Say no. Tell him that you made a mistake and that it's promised. She couldn't lie, and even if she did, he wouldn't believe her. "Yes."

"Good. I'll take it."

"For how long?"

Several heartbeats of silence followed during which Grace forced herself not to bite a hole in her lower lip.

"Couple days max."

"Fine."

A smile of sorts suddenly lightened his features. "I promise not to be any trouble."

"You'll be treated like all my other guests," she said as nonchalantly as possible.

"Fair enough."

Their gazes met again, and only by sheer force of will was Grace able finally to turn away.

"Yo, we're back."

Grace almost wilted visibly with relief at the timely arrival of the Brenners. "In the garden room," she called out.

When the elderly couple walked in and saw Denton, they pulled up short. "Sorry," Zelma said. "Are we interrupting anything?"

Grace smiled. "Of course not."

She introduced them, then watched as Denton smiled and shook their hands.

If ever two people appeared mismatched, it was Ed and Zelma. Ed was short and robust while Zelma was tall and thin. Though both were in their late seventies, they were full of boundless energy. Grace dreaded the day they left Ruby. She would miss them terribly, though they had already promised to return countless times.

"You're going to love your stay here, Mr. Hardesty," Zelma said, taking a seat across from Grace.

"I bet you're right about that," Denton said, smiling at Zelma.

Grace groaned inwardly as she watched him mesmerize the old lady. As a young man, he'd had plenty of charm. As a grown-up, he had perfected it and knew how to use it to his advantage.

With Ed and Zelma he was welcome to go all-out, to turn it on full blast if that would make him happy. As far as she was concerned, he was wasting his time. She planned to avoid him the entire length of his stay.

"Just wait till you taste her cooking," Ed was saying. "It's the best this side of heaven."

Zelma made an unladylike noise, though there was a twinkle in her eye as her gaze landed on her husband. "Are you saying I can't please you?"

"How would I know, honey bun? You haven't ever tried."

"Uh, right," Zelma said with a blush. "Well, are you ever in for a surprise."

He cut her a look. "I bet you can't cook."

"How'd you guess?"

They all chuckled, then Ed turned to Denton and asked, "You just passing through, young man?"

Grace looked on in silence as Denton explained about his vehicle. She tried not to concentrate on him, but it was hard. He was so easy to stare at she had to force her gaze away.

"Lucky man to have trouble in such an ideal spot," Ed responded. "We're both from Houston, but we're thinking about pulling up stakes and moving here."

Grace stared at them in amazement. "You are?"

"We're talking about it," Zelma said, sounding less enthusiastic.

Ed rested his gaze on Denton. "You couldn't ask for life any easier. It's sure nice not to hear the constant sounds of engines and horns. Instead you hear chirping birds and prattling insects."

"That's not Mr. Hardesty's cup of tea," Grace said without thought. "I'm sure he'll be bored with all that serenity."

Denton rested his intense gaze on her which made her want to squirm, but she didn't.

"I'm counting on you to see that doesn't happen," he said in an easy drawl, in contrast to her rather sharp one.

Ed and Zelma exchanged looks before bouncing their gazes between Grace and Denton as if picking up on the undercurrents in the room.

Deciding it was time to call a halt to this little chat, Grace stood. "Kitchen duty calls."

"I wish you'd let me help," Zelma said.

Grace shook her head. "Not a chance."

"Point me toward my room before you go, will you?" Denton asked, facing Grace.

"Now that I can do," Zelma said, claiming Denton's attention. "You just follow me."

"Thanks," Grace murmured, relieved she was spared being alone with Denton again. Her nerves were far too frayed to push her luck.

Ed shuffled toward them. "Wait for me."

Several minutes later Zelma walked back into the kitchen.

"What did he say?" Grace asked.

"He thanked me, then said he was going across the street to check on his car."

Grace merely nodded, her hands busy placing the fresh fruit on the tray.

"So what's with you two?" Zelma asked, a slight twitter in her tone.

Grace's head popped up. "I don't know what you're talking about."

"Now, honey, you can't fool this old fuddy-duddy. I know when electricity's crackling between two people."

"You're imagining things."

Zelma eyed her carefully. "I don't think so, but for now I'll mind my own business. But when you're ready to talk, I'm ready to listen." She paused with a wink. "I'll meet you back in the garden room."

Grace sagged against the counter, her heart beating far too hard and fast against her chest.

* * *

"It won't be long now, Mr. Hardesty, and I'll have you up and running."

Denton put his sunglasses on, then stared at the mechanic. "So you think you found the problem?"

"I know I have. It's just taking a tad longer than I thought to fix it."

"No problem. You take all the time you need."

Raymond gave him a puzzled look. "You mean you ain't in no hurry?"

"That's exactly what I mean."

Raymond rubbed his slightly grizzled chin. "Whatever you say."

Denton slapped a couple of bills in Raymond's hand then turned and headed back across the street.

A few minutes later he was opening the door to his room when a man strode by without so much as a nod. Strange-looking dude, Denton thought, comparing the stranger to someone out of a *Star Wars* movie. He was tall and thin to the point of gauntness. A hank of dark hair hung over his left eye.

He certainly didn't appear as if he belonged at Grace House, but then neither did he, Denton reminded himself scathingly.

Once he was in his room, he walked to the window and peered out at the front lawn. Though glorious beauty filled his vision, he failed to appreciate it, reaching into his pocket and pulling out a roll of antacids. After popping one in his mouth and chewing it, he released a deep sigh, then turned and stared at the antique four-poster bed with a step stool enabling a person to climb aboard. He smiled with no humor.

What the hell was he doing here? Had he lost his mind?

Yes.

No doubt about it: he'd taken complete leave of all his faculties. And why? Grace. It didn't take anyone with smarts to figure that out. Still, his actions made no sense.

Granted, when she'd opened the door, he'd felt as if he'd been hit upside the head with a crowbar. For some unknown reason, he'd assumed she hadn't hung around Ruby, either—that she'd flown the coop long ago. So much for that assumption. She'd not only remained but she'd gone into business here and apparently was very successful in her endeavor, which made him glad for her.

What a looker she'd turned into. Oh, she'd always been pretty, especially at eighteen, blessed with a natural beauty that few women could claim but all envied. That naturalness had stayed with her; only now it was enhanced by maturity and a hint of makeup.

Little else about her had changed, though, especially that delightful dimple. That had always captivated him and still did. He'd found himself wanting to dip his tongue in it the way he'd done so many times in the past.

A frown marred his face at the same time his loins stirred. Suddenly he fought the urge to grab another antacid, turn and get the hell out of there as fast as his legs could carry him. Yet he didn't move a muscle. It was as though his thoughts had him welded to the spot.

And that apron. He couldn't forget about that. He hadn't been making fun when he'd called attention to it, either. He'd been intrigued. And delighted. How quaint. How *uncitified*. But again, only someone with Grace's whimsical beauty and charm could pull it off.

The thought of any of his women friends donning an apron was so ludicrous he almost laughed out loud.

For his own peace of mind he wished Grace were married with 2.3 children and sported wrinkles and a little more fat. Instead she had remained thin, but not too thin, because her breasts seemed to fill her knit shirt to his standard of perfection.

Of course, her hair had changed. She now wore it in a short style that was a little edgy, a little messy. However, its color remained intact, the light-brown locks with blond streaks still contrasting sensationally with her dark eyes and luscious thick lashes.

She oozed a natural sexuality that he'd bet she wasn't even aware of. When he was in the room with her, he found it difficult to breathe. He was sure other men had been affected the same way.

So why had she been content to stagnate here where obviously there were no available men? No wonder she wasn't married. Suddenly he felt a small pinch of gladness at the thought, which was absurd since he was only passing through.

No matter. After he had walked out of her life the way he had, he was surprised she'd let him in the door. Maybe he'd been just as much a passing fancy for her as she'd been for him. Again it didn't matter. He had sworn off women, at least those with marriage in mind.

One wife, followed by a nasty divorce, was enough for him.

Yet he realized now more than ever that he'd never forgotten Grace or that night of passion they'd shared. He'd been nuts about her and hadn't wanted to leave her. He remembered that all too clearly. However, nothing had worked out according to either of their plans.

But that was then and this was now. He was no longer the horny college student who thought he'd die if he couldn't make her his, thinking he was in love. Lust. That was the emotion that had driven him. Love hadn't had anything to do with it, or so he'd convinced himself, having felt rotten at the outcome of their relationship.

"Damn," he muttered, reaching for another antacid.

This time there was no relief for the sour taste in his mouth and in his stomach. All he had to do was walk out of the room, tell Grace he couldn't stay, and that would be that. His life would be back on track once again, back to Dallas, back to his job.

And back to his nightmares about the plane crash that had brought him sleepless nights and restless days. Why had he been the only one spared that fateful day? He had walked away from the scattered debris and the mangled bodies of his best friend and the pilot.

It had been nearly a year since a malfunction in the engine had sent the small plane to the ground. Would the dark end of that bright spring day haunt him forever?

As if his body had suddenly become detached from his mind, Denton reached for his cell phone and punched in the number of his firm in Dallas.

Four

"See you later, dearie."

"I'm counting on that," Grace said, mustering up a sincere smile for Zelma.

Zelma winked, then whispered in a conspiratorial tone,"I'm going to join the old man for a late siesta."

This time Grace grinned openly. "Works for me."

Zelma's attractive features sobered. "You really ought to think about—"

"Don't you dare say it. Don't you dare think it."

"Oops, looks like I stepped in over my head again."

"Close to it," Grace countered, though her smile was back intact.

"It's just that you're so lovely, it's a shame—"

"Zelma!"

"I'm gone. I'm gone."

Once Grace was alone, she took a deep breath. She

knew Zelma meant well, that she wanted her to find and experience the kind of love that she and Ed shared. And while Grace appreciated that, she couldn't let Zelma think for one second that Denton might be the one.

A shiver darted through her. She had no intention of trekking down that rocky road again, though Zelma knew nothing of her and Denton's past and never would. Even so, she wasn't about to stand for Zelma's matchmaking, even if it was from the heart.

Grace glanced at the clock and saw that it was later than usual. But then, snack time had been later. Now, with the exception of Denton, the guests had all exited the garden room after having devoured the snack.

Since he'd returned from the gas station, he hadn't left his room. Most of the time he'd been on the phone. Because his room was the closest to the living areas, all had heard the sounds of his muffled voice. Although she couldn't decipher the exact words of his conversation and certainly didn't try, she had gotten the gist of them, anyway—all hell seemed to have broken loose in his office. No wonder he popped antacids as if they were going out of style.

What a dreadful way of life. Still, that was his choice, and he seemed to thrive on pressure. That was why she expected him to renege on his stay and leave at any time, regardless of his client and regardless of the status of his vehicle. She crossed her fingers that would be the case. Having him underfoot for even one night was not good. Seeing him again had affected her much more than she cared to admit. Her mind's eye suddenly conjured up the whipcord leanness of his body at the same time her senses smelled the slightly musky odor that was exclusively his.

And when he looked at her in that certain way, her entire body tingled. Stop it! she told herself. Stop adding fuel to an already smoldering fire. Those memories were not welcome. Besides, she could feel the anxiety building inside her, and she couldn't afford to let that happen. She'd been doing so well. No way was Denton Hardesty going to undermine that.

Suddenly unable to stand her idle hands, Grace scooped up the remains of snack time and almost ran into the kitchen. Keeping her momentum, she grabbed a bowl out of the cabinet, then crossed to the pantry where she latched on to a box of coffee cake mix, rationalizing that something different would be an extra attraction for tomorrow's breakfast. That way she could get ahead and keep her mind and hands occupied at the same time.

She was stirring the batter as if it was the enemy when she looked up and watched Zelma walk back in. "I thought you were taking a nap." Grace grinned. "Or something."

Zelma's mouth turned down. "Ed's snoring. What does that tell you?"

Grace's grin spread. "That you struck out."

"What's that you're whipping up on?" Zelma asked.

"Coffee cake."

"Ah, more fat for these hips."

"Pooh. You don't have an ounce of fat on you."

"Well, Ed does, but he's working on it."

"Think he'll forgive me for throwing temptation in his wake?"

"He won't forgive you if you don't."

They both chuckled, then Zelma said, "I came to see if you wanted to go dancing with us."

"Dancing?"

"Yeah, in Austin. We accidentally stumbled on a place that caters to old folks like us. Last week, though, there were several singles that joined in. So how about it?"

"Thanks, but I'll pass. It's been a long day."

Zelma eyed her curiously. "Are you sure?"

"I'm sure."

"Ah, come on and go. It'll do you good to shake a leg."

Both women turned and watched as Ed strolled in. Grace frowned, thinking something was not quite right about him, but she couldn't say what. For starters his color wasn't good; he looked almost pasty. She wondered if Zelma had picked up on that. Should she express her concern? No. It could just be her imagination which meant she would set off an alarm for nothing. But what if it wasn't?

"Ed, are you okay?" Grace asked.

"Yeah, honey," Zelma said, frowning in his direction. "You look—"

"I'm fine, sweetheart," Ed interrupted. He winked at Grace. "You're feeding me too good. That's the problem."

Still not convinced, but deciding to let the matter drop, Grace smiled. "So you two go ahead and shake all the legs you want. I'm heading for the bathtub."

"We'll see you later, then, hon," Ed said, taking Zelma's arm and steering her out.

Grace watched as they left the room, then turned her attention back to the cake batter, noticing that it had lumped on her. She began stirring it harder than ever.

"Why didn't you take them up on their offer?"

Grace's hands stilled, but her pulse didn't. It spiked to an all-time high. She raised her head. He was standing just inside the kitchen, looking and smelling much more appetizing than the cake batter in front of her. He had on a white knit shirt and a pair of casual slacks that left no doubt as to the strength of his muscles.

Judging from the dampness of his hair, he'd apparently just showered, which should have made him appear more rested. It didn't. It was obvious that he was tired, the grooves cutting deeper than ever into his eyes and mouth.

"I didn't want to dance, that's why," she finally said, dragging her gaze off him.

"It sounds like fun."

"I'm sure they'd let you tag along," she said for lack of anything better to say.

His lips quirked as he stepped closer. "I don't think so."

"Are you hungry?" she forced herself to ask. She had to dispel the sudden burgeoning tension.

"No, thanks."

"Just tired, huh?"

"Is it that obvious?"

"To me it is."

"Maybe that's because you know me so well."

Her eyes flared. "I don't know you at all."

"I haven't changed that much."

"Oh, please," she muttered, feeling as if she just stepped off into quicksand, and it was about to suck her under. But then that was the effect he'd always had on her from the first day she'd met him. Apparently, the years hadn't changed that, much to her chagrin.

"I like your kitchen."

His mentioning such a mundane thing was like being thrown a lifeline. She brightened and said, "Since I love to cook, I wanted it to be special."

And it was, with the large airy windows that went from ceiling to floor, letting in warmth and light and greenery from the outside. One seemed to be embraced the instant one walked in. Another attraction were the updated countertops and the polished hardwood cabinets.

"It feels like you've brought the outside in," Denton said, plopping down on the bar stool in front of her.

It was all Grace could do not to flinch visibly as his body seemed to envelop her. Unable to meet his direct gaze, she took a quivering breath, then pretended to stare outside. "I take that as a real compliment because that's exactly what I strove to do."

"So you decorated the house?"

His question drew her back around. "Most of it. Couldn't afford to hire anyone." Afraid she might sound as if she was whining, she added hastily, "But I wanted the responsibility, loved every minute of making this old place come back alive after sitting vacant for several years." She paused. "I'm not through, though, not by a long shot. There's so much else I want to do that needs to be done."

"I have faith in you," he said in a low tone.

Had that been his breath she felt caress her cheek? Swallowing against the clamoring going on inside her, she asked, "Sure you aren't hungry?"

"Depends."

"On what?"

"What you have to offer."

She expelled a shaky breath but it did little to relieve the pressure inside her. He was deliberately toying with her emotions. But if she hit him with that accusation, he'd deny it. Or would he?

God, what an intolerable situation. Drawing back, she said, in what she hoped was a perfectly normal but standoffish tone, "I have some cold cuts, salad—"

"Thanks but no thanks," he said abruptly.

She watched as he reached in his pocket and pulled out his pack of antacids.

"That's obviously your diet of choice."

His lips thinned as he rubbed the back of his neck in a gesture of frustration. "It gets the job done."

"I hope the job's worth it," she said, holding on to her normal tone, though it was hard, especially when she wanted to reach out and touch those grooves in his forehead, soothe them away. Then, realizing where her thoughts had wandered, she shut them down.

"It is." His tone was definitely clipped.

"Did I hit an exposed nerve?"

He scowled. "So you obviously don't like pressure. Well, I do. Otherwise, I'd be bored."

"Good luck."

His eyes narrowed. "What does that mean?"

"On convincing yourself."

A smile of sorts softened his lips. "You don't pull any punches, do you? Okay, so things aren't going so well right now. I'll admit that."

"The boss is not happy you're here." It was a statement of fact.

Denton's laugh was humorless. "That's putting it mildly."

She didn't dare ask him when he was leaving. She didn't want him to go, but she was afraid for him to stay. And why that was so, she dared not ask herself. Having him in front of her, within touching distance but not touching him, was playing havoc with her emotions, a complication she didn't need or deserve.

"So, is making more money your goal?"

He almost smiled again. "That and making partner in the firm."

"I guess that makes Mummy and Daddy proud." She had purposely avoided asking about his parents, whom she partly blamed for their breakup. They had never liked her, never thought she was good enough for their son. However, she couldn't blame then totally. Denton could have bucked them, but he hadn't. He'd gone right along with his dad's wishes. Then his dad had had a stroke, which had further complicated matters.

"Sarcasm doesn't become you," he said, drawing her back to the moment at hand.

"Is that on the horizon? Becoming partner, I mean?" she said, deliberately changing the subject.

"It'd better be. If I nail this client, then I feel I'm a shoo-in."

"Then I hope it happens."

He delved into her eyes. "You don't mean that."

She flushed, stirring harder. "You're doing it again."

"What?" he asked in a innocent tone.

Innocent, hell. He'd never been innocent. "Assuming you can read my mind."

"What are you making?" he asked, his tone having dropped to a sultry pitch deep in the danger zone.

"Uh, a cake," she responded, clearly thrown off-kilter by his unexpected change in subject.

He chuckled suddenly, and his eyes heated.

Her system went haywire. "What's...so funny?"

"You've got a glob of batter on your face."

Before she could respond, a finger reached out and scooped it off. Then, without removing his hot gaze, he deliberately licked his finger, making a sucking noise.

The bottom dropped out of her stomach.

Five

He should've kept his hands to himself, dammit. He didn't know what had possessed him. Yes, he did. That same old lust, smoldering deep in his gut had spurred him into action. Too, she'd looked so delightful with that glob of batter on her cheek, almost dead center on the dimple, that he couldn't resist touching her.

No excuse.

That gesture was bad enough, but to deliberately lick the goo off his finger had earned him a swift kick in the butt. For a second he'd even been tempted to kiss her. However, his sound senses had come to his rescue, taunting him with the realization that actions good or bad had consequences. He'd pulled back.

His mood darkening, Denton strode to the bedside table and stared at his cell phone. He ought to call Dallas, more specifically his boss Todd Joseph. But not right now, he argued. He wasn't in the mood to intentionally put himself in front of a firing squad.

At the moment he was feeling more vulnerable, more exposed than he had since the crash. Not a good feeling.

Maybe seeing his client today and sealing a deal would help him regain some of his perspective and sanity. For some reason, both seemed to have deserted him, or he would never have stayed the night here when he'd had plenty of other choices.

Grace.

She was the reason he hadn't left. It was as simple as that. Only it apparently wasn't that simple or his gut wouldn't be twisted in a knot or his mouth as dry as a pine knot. When she had opened that door yesterday, he'd been suckered in again like days of old. He'd thought about her all night, and even now at dawn thirty, he couldn't stop thinking about her.

Nothing had happened, for God's sake, he kept telling himself, sounding like a damn broken record, or rather a teenager in heat.

He *hadn't* kissed her. He'd only touched her and very briefly at that. He was making it a much bigger deal than it was. At this rate he'd be a candidate for the rubber room if he were to get mixed up with Grace again.

It was obvious from her reaction to his touch that they were on the same page. Her eyes had widened, and she had flinched as if he'd struck her. However, he was barely conscious of her reaction, since he was so busy trying to control and mask his own turbulent emotions.

He'd experienced an instant tightening behind his zipper, and his breath had jammed in his throat.

"You don't care who you hurt, do you?" she'd said in a tight, quavering voice, her troubled eyes meeting his.

"Grace, I—"

"I don't want you to say anything. Just know that I'm not the innocent I once was and that I can see you for who and what you are."

That time he'd flinched, her words having cut to the core, because he knew what she said was the truth even though he hated to admit that even to himself.

"I never meant to—"

Again she'd stopped him in a voice that was colder than chips of ice. "Let it be, Denton. Now, if you don't mind, I'd like to finish the cake."

In other words, go take a hike was what she'd told him. And while he'd thought about calling her hand and pushing his luck, he hadn't. She'd already made him feel like pond scum. Why stick around and beg for more?

He had left and gone to his room where he'd worked on several reports until the wee hours of the morning, having thought to grab his briefcase out of the trunk when he'd checked on his BMW. He hadn't even bothered to climb on the big bed. Instead he'd taken a couple of catnaps on the chaise lounge.

That was why he felt as if he'd been drawn and quartered this morning, though he suspected his exhaustion was as much mental as physical. After a hot shower, he'd feel better, more like facing the day and the responsibilities that it would bring.

Forget her.

Once he left town that would be easy enough to do. And once he was back home on his own turf, everything would shift back in sync. He'd forget all about this trip down memory lane. Most of all he'd forget about Grace, forget her infectious smile, the delectable curve of her breasts, the "come hither" sway of her hips. What he wouldn't forget, however, were her lips, how that lower one was fuller, how it protruded just enough to make him want to take it in his own and suck it.

Denton groaned as a shaft of heat surged through him, so intense that it almost buckled his knees. He took several deep breaths, then practically fell onto the chaise and closed his eyes.

No relief.

Grace had managed to invade his space to the extent that she was imprinted on his brain. Déjà vu. That was what this was all about, the memory of their last time together suddenly burning a destructive trail through his memory.

They had begun dating toward the end of her senior year in high school, his second year at Stanford. He'd come home for the summer to work and take some classes at the University of Texas.

He had met Grace at a friend's party. From the beginning he'd been smitten. He'd taken her home from the shindig, and that was it. He couldn't leave her alone. They had been together every evening, despite the fact that his parents objected, thinking he was getting much too serious about someone whom they saw as a threat to their son's bright future.

Denton ignored their pleas, knowing he couldn't leave her alone even if he'd wanted to. Still, he'd kept his head, knowing his limits—until that night. Since he was returning to Stanford the following day, he had taken her on a picnic to his parents' farm so they could have complete privacy.

It had been a lovely spring day much like yesterday. They had consumed a lot of food and drink and had fallen asleep on the blanket.

He had been the first to awaken, watching as the sun slowly turned its reign of power over to the moon. He had nuzzled her awake with his tongue, first in her ear, then her cheek, and finally her mouth.

A pleasurable moan had escaped through her lips as she'd opened her eyes and pulled his face closer. "Don't leave tomorrow," she whispered. "Please."

"God, I don't want to," he said, his tone filled with agony. "I can't stand the thought of not seeing you for weeks."

"Then don't go."

"My parents would kill me."

He dipped his tongue in her mouth and for a moment tongues sparred gently. Then his hands found and kneaded her breasts before unbuttoning her blouse. She didn't have on a bra, which didn't surprise him since she knew how much he loved to touch her breasts.

After tweaking both nipples, he leaned over and began sucking them.

She squirmed, her hand reaching for his crotch where she rubbed up and down, something she'd done on numerous occasions without him losing control. Instead he would use his tongue and lips to full advantage, confident he brought her complete and intense satisfaction, not worrying about himself until later.

But that evening it was especially difficult to hold himself in check, maybe because he knew he wasn't going to see her for a while. Or maybe it was because he wanted her so desperately.

"Make love to me," she whispered, her voice raspy and pleading.

"Grace, you know I want to, that I'm dying to be inside you."

"Then what's stopping you?"

"You know." He frowned. "What if you got pregnant?"

"I won't."

"How can you be so sure?"

"I'm taking the Pill."

He sucked in his breath and stared hard at her. "Since when?"

"Since long enough for them to take effect."

"Grace, I—"

"Shh, I don't want a lecture, I want you."

It was then that she snuck her hand down in his running shorts and surrounded him. Within seconds they were both naked, his lips and hands all over her. Only after he feared he would explode in her hand did he ease inside her, instantly hitting a barrier.

Cursing, he tried to pull out, but she clung to him.

"It's...okay," Grace said breathlessly. "It'll be all right. I want you so...much."

He thrust into her then, crushing her against him....

At first Denton wasn't sure what was ringing, his head or his phone. Nonetheless, his eyes popped open and he bounded off the chaise as if he'd been shot. Following several hard-won breaths, he realized it was his cell.

He grabbed it like a lifeline, sweat pouring off him. Gritting his teeth, he flipped the lid. "Hardesty."

"Your ass had better be headed this way."

"Good morning to you, too."

"Don't you 'good morning' me," Todd snapped.

If Denton hadn't had such a hard-on, literally, he would've laughed. In his mind's eye, he could see his friend and soon-to-be partner in his chair with his feet propped on his desk, chomping down on that unlit cigar stuck in one corner of his mouth. A disgusting habit, Denton never failed to tell him every chance he got. No matter—Todd continued to cram it between his lips.

"Chomp a little harder on that cigar," Denton advised. "That'll take some of the pressure off."

"What the hell's going on?"

"I'm seeing my client today."

"You should've come back yesterday, then gone back."

"That's crazy. Besides, my car is out of commission."

"Well, all hell's breaking loose here."

"The money we're going to get from this deal will glue things back together real quick."

"If you nail it."

"Oh, I'll nail it, all right. Look, I'll see you this evening."

"You damn well better."

With that Todd slammed down the receiver. If it had been anyone else, Denton would've been livid. But Todd, like him, marched to his own drummer. You either tolerated him or you didn't. Denton chose to tolerate him, as he was one intelligent cookie and knew more about investments and the stock market than the Japanese.

Hanging with Todd, despite his idiosyncrasies, would make him a rich man before he was forty if he made partner, which he was determined to do. That was why he had to get the hell away from Grace. She was messing with his mind, and he couldn't allow that.

Still sweating, he headed for the bathroom as his cell rang again. He was tempted not to answer it, thinking it was probably Todd calling back to further harass him. But he couldn't take a chance. He had several deals pending.

He answered it, only then to halt in his tracks and stifle a curse.

Did she look as bad as she felt?

Probably worse, she told herself. But what could she expect when she hadn't closed her eyes the entire night? She did indeed look worse than she felt, though she'd tried to mask the dark circles under her eyes with a stick of concealer, a product she rarely used. Extra blush and lipstick had given her little satisfaction.

At least her outfit was presentable. She'd chosen a pair of khaki capri pants that molded her slender frame and a pink knit top that did the same. Right in step with spring, she told herself sarcastically, wondering why she cared how she looked.

After this morning she would never see him again.

A tight squeeze inside her chest took her breath. If only he hadn't touched her. If only he hadn't looked at her with such smoldering desire. And when he'd blatantly licked his finger, heat had pooled between her legs, something she hadn't experienced in years. When he had walked out of the kitchen, she'd felt wrung out and still did.

But it would all be over shortly. She didn't look for him to appear at breakfast, which would be a blessing. She would have to face him when he tried to pay her, only she had no intention of charging him, even though she could use the money.

She just wanted him out of her life before she did something stupid and let him kiss her, or worse. Once he was gone, the sexual longings he'd aroused in her would go dormant again, the way she wanted them. Until then, she'd just have to endure the moistness between her legs and her distended nipples.

She had prepared most of the breakfast and set the table when he walked in, looking as if he'd fought the same bear she had. Good. Misery loved company. Too, he deserved whatever he got for opening that sealed can of worms.

Yet, she fought the urge to run to him and fling her arms around him. Just one more time.

"Mornin'," he said into the silence, avoiding her gaze.

Grace nodded. "Are you joining us for breakfast?" she asked without preamble. Of course he wasn't. But as hostess she had to ask.

"As a matter of fact, I am."

She gave a start. "But I thought—"

"Me, too, only there's been a change of plans."

"Oh." The tiny word was barely audible.

This time his gaze met hers directly. "I need to stay a few more days. Do you mind?"

Six

In a hunter-green T-shirt and casual khaki slacks, his dark hair once again damp and slightly mussed, he looked big, sleek and undeniably sexy. And totally out of place in *her* kitchen, in *her* life. That was why he had to leave. She couldn't allow him to stay and continue to disrupt her routine.

After her sleepless night, she hadn't as yet gotten her act together. Hence breakfast was going to be a few minutes late, and that didn't sit well with her. Not only was she a stickler for time but for perfection. With Denton around, nothing was on schedule. Certainly nothing was perfect.

"Well?"

"I don't think that's a good idea."

"Why not?"

Her temper rose. "Don't treat me like I'm an imbecile."

He blew out a breath, and his eyes narrowed. "That's not what I intended, and you know it."

"I don't know any such thing."

"Okay, so I was out of line. I'm sorry."

Maybe he was sorry, but that didn't change anything. However, unless she was prepared to have an all-out verbal slinging match with him, which she was not, she'd best take hold of her fractured emotions and handle this volatile situation as best she could.

"Look, there are other places—"

"Is the room spoken for?" he interrupted.

That was when she noticed his exhaustion. His eyes were bloodshot and his lips were stretched in a thin line. When he'd first walked in, his sexual charisma had overpowered her, and that was all she'd noticed. Now she realized he must've had a night comparable to hers. Only she didn't kid herself that his restlessness pertained to her, but to Dallas and his job.

So why didn't he just go back there?

"Grace, answer me."

Her brain buzzed while she stalled for time. "Er, no, it's not."

"Then I'd like to have it for at least several more days."

Oh, dear Lord, no. She'd be a fool to let him stay any longer. "Why?" she asked, then colored, having realized that was none of her business. She would never have asked another guest that question. But Denton wasn't just another guest, she reminded herself. He was an unwelcome memory from her past.

"My prospective client's still out of town, won't be back for several more days."

"You don't have to return to Dallas?" Again she was treading on unprofessional ground, but she didn't care. If he minded, then he could leave, which is what she wanted. Didn't she?

He walked toward her, not stopping until he reached the stove where she stood preparing breakfast. He placed an arm on the countertop as though to brace himself. She felt his eyes probing, but she dared not look at him. Besides, she was suddenly mesmerized by his hands, by the coarse dark hair that dusted his skin.

"I should get back to the office, only I'm not," he said in a raspy tone.

She didn't respond right off, still too conscious of him, his nearness suffocating in its intensity.

"Grace, I'm not going to hurt you."

At those softly spoken words, her head whipped up, and their gazes slammed together. It was as if she'd been hit by an electric shock. She knew that he'd felt it, too, as he released an unsteady breath and stepped back.

"You'll never get that chance again, Denton. Trust me on that."

He flushed. "I deserve your contempt and more."

"Look, I have to get breakfast."

"So do I get the room or not?"

Still she hesitated.

"Do you want me to beg?"

"Of course not," she muttered tersely. "And you wouldn't, either."

"Don't count on it."

A shiver darted through her. What kind of game was he playing? More to the point, why was she letting him play it?

"Yes or no."

"You sure you wouldn't rather I call another B&B?"

"I'm positive," he said, his eyes probing once again.

"Oh, all right," she said ungraciously.

"Did it hurt that badly?"

A smile was now toying with his lips which lessened the tension considerably. She even took a clear breath as she once again busied her hands with placing the biscuits on an oven tray. Thank goodness she'd already prepared the scrambled eggs, gravy and grits. They were in the warmer, waiting to be served. The fruit cups were also filled and in the frig.

"No, I guess it didn't," she finally admitted, though she couldn't quite muster a smile.

"Is there anything I could do to help?" he asked.

"Like what?"

A genuine smile broke through his lips. "Hey, I can cook."

"As in popping TV dinners in the micro," she responded, hating the way her pulse reacted to that smile.

"I can fix beans and corn bread. Does that count?"

"Not this morning."

He chuckled. "Well, I could—"

"Cut some flowers for the table."

"You got it," he said, suddenly sounding like a youngster who was eager to please.

Not good. Not good at all, at least not for her peace of mind, she told herself, all the while raking herself over the coals for giving in to his demand to board him for several more days. Later, she knew she'd really be in a state. Now, however, it was imperative she act as if he were just another guest, no one special.

Holding a sigh in check, Grace reached into a nearby drawer. "Here's a pair of scissors, and the vase is in the top of that cabinet."

"Any particular brand you want?"

Her lips twitched at his terminology. "It's your call."

He stared at her a moment longer then turned and strode out the French doors, an added bounce to his steps. Grace, on the other hand, leaned against the counter, feeling limp like all the air had been let out of her body.

She'd lost her mind. That was all there was to it. She should've told him to get lost. Instead, she'd committed the unpardonable—she'd let her heart overrule her head, one more time.

Grace fought the sudden urge to untie her apron and take flight herself. If he wouldn't go, then she would. That thought was absurd, of course. Still, the urge refused to go away, and she felt tears festering behind her eyes.

She didn't want them to wander down that old familiar path; she didn't want to feel this disturbing softening towards him. She wanted only to remember how badly he'd hurt her, how he'd crushed her heart into tiny pieces that had never quite mended despite the passing years.

Yet here he was back in her life, back in her house, for heaven's sake. But not in her bed. Never that. If he so much as tried to touch her again, she'd—

"Who's that good-looking specimen messing in the flower garden?"

Zelma's presence was a heartfelt relief to her battered thoughts. "Denton Hardesty." She forced her tone to remain generic.

"Ah, the man I met yesterday."

Grace nodded.

"So he's still here." A flat statement of fact.

"For a few more days."

"Mmm."

"Zip up your mind, my friend."

Zelma laughed. "Whatever you say. Ah, here comes that sweet husband of mine."

"Good morning," Ed said, leaning over and kissing Grace on the cheek. "How's my other girl?"

Grace smiled, glad to see that Ed seemed to be feeling much better. "I'm about to serve you something to eat." She paused. "How was your outing last night?"

Before either could answer, Ralph Kennedy ambled into the kitchen. "Am I too early?" he asked, looking his usual uncomfortable self.

"You're just right," Grace said. "Go ahead and take your seat in the dining room."

What a strange person, she thought again as she smiled in at him, hoping to put him at ease. She had thought her hearty morning meals would have put some meat on his gaunt frame by now, but so far they hadn't. If anything, he appeared more skeletal than when he first came. This morning his glasses were perched on the bridge of his nose indicating he had already been hard at work.

Denton chose that moment to walk in with a vase filled with an incredible array of tulips.

"Oh, Mr. Hardesty, how gorgeous."

He turned on his high-wattage smile on Zelma. "Make that Denton, ma'am."

"As long as you call us Zelma and Ed."

Grace formally introduced Ralph to Denton before they all took their place at the table. Grace began serving immediately, finding that her hands were quite steady despite the fact that she sensed rather than saw Denton's eyes track her every move.

All in all, breakfast turned out to be a fun time. Denton held court and all seemed to enjoy his anecdotes, even Ralph, which surprised Grace. She didn't recall ever having heard him laugh.

Soon, however, the meal was completed and everyone left the dining room with the exception of Denton. She was back in the kitchen at the sink when she sensed he'd joined her. She swung around.

"Need some help with the dishes?" he asked.

She picked up on the note of uncertainty in his tone, realizing he was at loose ends and didn't know what to do with time on his hands. But that was his problem, not hers. He should've taken that into consideration when he decided to remain in town. If he thought she was going to entertain him, he was in for a rude awakening.

"No, thanks. My part-time help will be here shortly."

"I could pitch in till then."

She expelled a sigh, then muttered, "Go sightseeing."

"That's a nice way of saying get lost, right?"

She flushed but didn't flinch.

He stepped forward, his gaze trapping hers, then in a low, tortured voice he whispered, "I dreamed about us making love last night."

Grace was bone tired, but, like the night before, sleep eluded her. She'd had a hot bath and a warm glass of milk. Neither had taken the edge off her nerves. Maybe she should go talk to Zelma. Her eyes went to the clock on the table next to her chaise lounge. Ten o'clock.

By her usual standards that was early, but with her exhaustion being at such a high level, ten was late. She hated to disturb Zelma. Anyway, what could she tell her? Nothing. She wasn't about to divulge her past with Denton, so what would be the point?

For one thing she couldn't stand to be alone with her thoughts. Denton and only Denton filled her mind to capacity. After he had told her he'd dreamed about them making love, her body had gone into instant meltdown and hadn't recovered.

"Go away and leave me alone," she'd said, lashing back at him.

"Dammit, Grace, you just don't get it, do you?"

"I don't want to get it."

"I stayed because I thought—"

"Thought what? That we might just play footsie in bed again?"

His face went white. "I just thought—" He broke off and rubbed the back of his neck in a frustrated gesture. "Oh, hell, I don't know what I thought."

"You didn't think."

"Do you hate me that much?"

"Yes," she lied.

He sucked in a harsh breath. "Then I guess that says it all."

Before she could come up with a suitable comeback, he turned and marched out of the room.

Now as she sat alone in her room, Grace wished she could recall those bitter words, tone them down a bit. Okay, so she'd like to make love to him again, too.

Just the thought sent a fiery warmth spreading through her body. It had been a long time since she'd been with a man. And when she had, it hadn't been a pleasant experience.

Only Denton had brought her the sexual satisfaction she craved. And since she couldn't have him, she'd decided to do without.

Then Denton had waltzed back into her life. And if she so chose, she could have him back in her bed. But at what price? One she wasn't willing to pay.

Holding on to that thought, Grace switched off the lamp and made her way back to bed.

At first she wasn't sure what awakened her. Her eyes suddenly opened wide. Then she heard the noise again. A scream. A bloodcurdling scream, at that. It sounded like Zelma.

With her heart pounding out of her chest, Grace tossed back the sheet and ran out of the room into the hallway. Denton, with only a pair of running shorts on, met her there.

"What the hell?" he asked.

"Screams coming from Ed and Zelma's room."

Together they ran down the hall as another scream rent the air.

Grace reached the door first and thrust it open, then pulled up short, causing Denton to slam into her. Following a muttered curse, he righted her with hands on both her arms. She was hardly aware of the contact as her eyes were filled with the image in front of her. Zelma was cradling Ed's seemingly lifeless body in her arms, rocking back and forth.

"I...I think he's gone," she whispered, focusing tear-stained eyes on Grace.

Seven

"**I** can't believe he's not gone."

"Hey," Denton said to Zelma, holding her against his side and squeezing her thin body for a moment. "He's going to pull out of this. I won't pretend it's not serious, because it is. However, he's a determined man, and that makes a difference. Anyway, he's not about to give up and leave you to run the streets of that big city alone."

"Oh, Denton, I can't thank you and Grace enough. I don't—" Zelma's voice cracked, and she couldn't go on.

"Shh, don't get yourself all worked up again." Denton smiled down at her before gently pushing her away. "You'll be in the bed next to him if you don't buck up."

"He'd have another attack if that happened," Zelma said with a semblance of a smile.

Grace looked on, thinking how wonderful, how like a rock Denton had been throughout this entire ordeal. Had it just been three hours ago that Zelma's frantic cry had jerked the entire B&B awake? It seemed as if she'd been up several days without sleep. Her eyes felt filled with sand.

Denton wasn't faring much better, appearing equally as weary. But he didn't let on for a second that he might be running out of energy or confidence. She didn't know what she would've done if he hadn't been there. Oh, she would have coped; she would not have had any choice. However, it wouldn't have been easy, given her past problems and Zelma's hysteria.

As they waited for the doctors to return to the hospital waiting room and update them on Ed's condition, Grace uncurled her legs, stood and stretched. For some reason she chose that second to look at Denton. He was watching her, his eyes on her jutting breasts, breasts that were bra free.

Instantly Grace felt her nipples tighten and thrust against the thin fabric of her blouse. She knew that Denton saw them, too, as heat suddenly leaped into his eyes, darkening them. For a second she couldn't move, heat surging through her own body as their gazes met and held.

She deliberately jerked her eyes off him and back to Zelma who was standing with her back to them, facing the lit parking lot outside. Purposely, Grace walked up next to Zelma and placed her arm around her.

"Oh, Gracie, I'm so frightened."

"I wish you'd let me call your kids."

"If he's not really better, then we will," Zelma said. "I promise. But they all live so far away."

"Like Denton said, he's going to make it."

"You're right, he is."

All eyes whipped around and faced the small and rather rotund doctor who was smiling at them. "He had a heart attack for sure, though the damage to his heart muscle is minimal."

"Oh, Doctor, praise the Lord," Zelma cried.

"We're going to keep him overnight, of course, and part of tomorrow, and run some more tests to see just how much blockage he has. Then you can take him home."

"Thank you so much, Doctor," Denton said, stepping forward and shaking his hand."

"Mrs. Brenner, you may see him now."

Once Zelma had left, the tiny waiting room in the cardiac unit fell silent as a tomb. Grace wrapped both arms around herself to keep herself from shaking. She couldn't lose it now, not when the crisis was past. Thank God Ed hadn't died and was going to actually get well.

"Are you okay?"

Denton's low, raspy voice brought her around to face him. "No," she said honestly.

"Didn't think so."

"How 'bout you?"

"Don't worry about me. I deal with one crisis or another every day, though someone's life doesn't hang in the balance. But you'd think it did, the way some of my clients carry on."

Grace shuddered visibly. "I'd hate that."

"Sometimes I do."

"Then why don't you do something else?"

An eyebrow shot up. "How did we get onto me?

It's you who looks like you're going to drop any minute."

Grace gnawed at her lower lip and when she spoke, her voice wasn't quite steady. "I haven't slept much lately."

"Me, neither."

For another long moment their eyes met and held.

"Grace," he muttered, stepping forward.

"Hey, you two, Ed's asking for you. Follow me."

The unexpected sound of Zelma's voice shattered the spell, though Grace continued to shake on the inside, fighting off the crazy feeling that Denton had just kissed her.

She shivered again.

His BMW was repaired, washed and polished until it shone like new money and was waiting to be driven. Standing at the window the following morning, Denton could see it. It was almost as if it was beckoning him.

So why didn't he walk outside, jump in it and haul it back to Dallas?

The bottom line was that he was enjoying the relaxed atmosphere, the chance to slow down and smell the roses, the main rose being Grace, even though plucking that rose was off-limits. But he needed this time. He'd earned it.

Still, in his gut he knew he had no business whatsoever lollygagging around Ruby any longer. It was a given that Grace didn't want him here, though he knew she wasn't as immune to him as she'd like to be. He'd seen matching fire in her eyes when she'd caught his gaze locked on her jutting nipples.

But looking was as far as he would ever get. He

might as well accept that and move on. And since Ed was out of immediate danger, he wasn't needed here.

But he was needed in the office. He should return to Dallas, then drive back to meet his client. Simple solution.

Hell, driving was no big deal. He put thousands of miles on a vehicle each year since his clients were spread all over the country. What was a big deal was his absence from the office. He didn't know how much longer Todd was going to humor him before he went on the warpath. He did that often when he didn't get his way.

Denton hadn't called and told him he'd decided to cool his heels and take a few days of his vacation, something he'd never done since he started with the firm years ago. He'd often thought his penchant for work had helped bring about the demise of his marriage.

Once he and Marsha had split up, he'd rarely thought of her, a fact he considered odd. It was almost as if that time in his life had been a dream rather than a reality. They simply hadn't had enough in common, or spent enough time together, which was his fault. He'd felt that he had to get ahead, make it big. His parents had drilled success into him, stressing that money was the measuring stick for one's success.

He no longer thought that, yet he hadn't been able to get off the fast track. Until now. And he had Grace to thank for such a remarkable about-face, though he couldn't share that with her. Right now, if he even looked at her, she seemed to panic, not visibly, but he could see it in her eyes, in the way she froze up.

Her reaction was his fault, too. He would give anything to right that old wrong, but he didn't know how.

He wanted her, in his arms, in his bed. He wouldn't deny his need, not even to her. There was something about her, about them, that was explosive. He couldn't explain it, but he didn't see it ever changing, not after all this time.

He was as infatuated as if the years had never passed. Watching her work in the kitchen, watching her do anything, made him want her just one more time.

However, he wasn't looking for a serious relationship. Not now, not ever. Hell, he was too big a mess to take on the responsibility of someone else. Since the plane crash, he'd done some crazy things. Remaining in Ruby for no reason other than desire was probably the craziest yet.

A harsh sigh escaped Denton as he massaged his neck where tight ridges of muscles didn't want to give.

Making love to Grace would do the trick, bring relief to his aching muscles and his manhood. Then what? She wasn't the one-night-stand kind of woman. And if he ever made love to her again, he doubted he could walk. That thought alone jarred him to the core.

So the answer was to keep his zipper zipped and his head on straight.

"Give it a rest," Denton spat, the sound of his voice bouncing off the walls.

God, everything was so quiet, a novelty for him, certainly something he wasn't used to. Right now the solitude was what his battered senses needed. With that thought in mind, he made his way out of his room and into the kitchen.

Empty.

Where was Grace? He'd missed breakfast, which

was not important. He was used to drinking his morning meal, his gaze targeting the coffee urn, then making a beeline for it.

He had just poured himself a full mug when he saw Grace through the window, traipsing toward the vegetable garden. How fresh and lovely she looked this bright spring morning, dressed in a purple T-shirt, white walking shorts and white tennis shoes with no socks. But it was the straw hat perched on top of her head just right that made him chuckle out loud.

The women he knew wouldn't be caught dead in a hat. Hell, they wouldn't be caught dead working in a garden. Of any kind. He watched, fascinated, as she pulled a pair of gloves out of her pocket, put them on, then dropped to her knees.

By God, she was going to weed the garden.

Not without his help, she wasn't, he told himself, making his way to the door as fast as he could.

"Hey, Z, I'm so glad you called," Grace said. "I was afraid to call you for fear of disturbing Ed."

"He's doing great, honey. We talked to all the kids."

"Talked them out of coming, I'll bet," Grace said.

"Of course, we did. We're coming home in the morning."

Grace felt a warm feeling flood through her when Zelma referred to the B&B as home. What a compliment to her. "Does he have to behave himself?"

Zelma laughed. "He can't dance the jitterbug right off, but he can dance."

Jitterbug. Grace rolled her eyes, thinking she'd have trouble jitterbugging, and she was eons younger. She bet Denton could. Suddenly her face lost its animation. She didn't want to start her morning off thinking about *him*.

But she might as well have as Zelma's next question concerned him.

"So how's our knight in shining armor?"

If she only knew. "I haven't seen him."

"Oh? Well, when you do, tell him again how much we appreciate him and what he did. You, too, but that goes without saying."

"I'll tell him."

There was a short pause, then Zelma said, "You wouldn't consider giving him a hug for me, would you?"

"Zelma," Grace muttered, "don't push your luck, okay?"

"All right, my dear. Oops, gotta go. The doctor just came in. I'll talk to you later."

Once the receiver was back in place, Grace peered at the clock. With the Brenners' absence and Denton having no interest in breakfast, she'd prepared a tray and taken it to Ralph's room, a gesture he seemed to appreciate as he was trying desperately to finish his novel on time.

Now she had extra time of her own and didn't know what to do with it. She did know, however, that she had to keep busy or she'd go nuts. Having Denton under her roof continued to unnerve her.

Okay, so she still hadn't gotten over him, dammit. Okay, so he had the power to turn her bones to butter when he looked at her. Okay, so he didn't even have to look at her; he just had to walk into the same room.

She was smitten. Still.

But that would change, she told herself. Thank God she no longer loved him. Her fixation was loneliness and lust. But those were a disastrous combination. Hopefully this time her recovery period would be much shorter. Her heart knew they had no future, that he merely wanted to make love to her, then walk away like before.

They were from two different worlds, and that wasn't going to change. Nor did she want it to. She couldn't survive in the city and he couldn't survive in the country. But their differences went much deeper than locale.

She had known the boy. She didn't know the man.

"Grrrrh!" she muttered, suddenly feeling claustrophobic, knowing she had to get out of the house.

A few minutes later she headed for the garden. She was halfway there when she sensed she was being watched. She didn't know how or why. She would have to credit her gut instinct.

Denton. It was him. Her instinct was on high alert.

Unable to stop her heart from racing, she bent down and attacked the weeds without mercy, not even looking up when she saw him leave the house and stride toward her.

"I know you won't refuse my help *this* morning."

Eight

He strolled into the garden where she'd been weeding, and without waiting for her permission to help, he dropped to his knees and began jerking out the weeds right alongside her. Her breathing had become so erratic she feared he could hear it.

"Do you always do just what you want?" she finally said into the building silence.

He turned and cut her a lopsided smile, sweat already dotting his forehead and upper lip. "If I think it's necessary."

"And you thought this was necessary, huh?"

"Yep, since there's more weeds than flowers." His grin widened. "Besides, you have no idea how long it's been since I've had my hands in dirt."

This time she chuckled. She couldn't help herself. "I bet if your colleagues back in the office could see you now they would think you'd lost it."

"Probably, but then what they don't know won't hurt them. Right?"

"Uh, right."

"How 'bout the vegetables?" He angled his head in the direction of the adjacent vegetable patch. "They're in as bad a shape. Or worse."

Grace pushed back her hat and wiped at her forehead. That was when she realized he was watching her again, his eyes piercing. And still he was so close—almost shoulder to shoulder close.

"Did I tell you how great you look in that hat?"

Her face flooded with color, but she hoped he wouldn't notice. Or if he did, he'd think it was the heat rather than his huskily spoken compliment. "Are you making fun?" Her voice quavered slightly.

"No, I mean it. It makes you look—" he broke off and smiled "—I don't know. Younger maybe, like a girl." Then he flapped a dirty hand in the air. "Hell, I don't know. I just like it. It's kind of like your apron—it's just you."

"Quaint."

"Why are you always putting yourself down?"

"I'm not," she snapped, jerking out as much dirt as weeds. "I think this town and I are just jokes to you, something you can and will chuckle about when you get back to your highfalutin office."

"I don't think so."

"I hope not," she said, "because my life, including cooking and gardening, brings me the greatest of pleasure."

"Hey, again, you don't have to convince me. I'm on your side. If I had an outlet like this maybe I—"

"Wouldn't be continually eating antacids like candy."

He didn't so much as flinch at her directness. In fact, he smiled, which made her heart turn over. "Can't argue with the truth."

As if she'd really given him food for thought, they worked in silence until Grace had to stand; her legs were beginning to cramp from being in one position for so long. While Denton hadn't looked the least uncomfortable, he was sweating profusely despite the fact the near-temperature was only in the low eighties. The bad guy was the humidity. It was high today, rare for the hill country.

Denton also stood, wiped the sweat off his face with a handkerchief from his back pocket, then asked, "Shall we hit the veggies next?"

"Are you serious?"

"Sure. Why not?"

"Look, I really appreciate your help, but—"

"Hey, lighten up, okay? I don't have anything else to do. But even if I did, I'd want to help."

"You always did have a green thumb. I'd forgotten until now."

"Me, too," he said in a low voice tinged with regret.

"Well, if you're serious, let's get to it," Grace said, that breathlessness back in her voice. But as long as he was sharing her space, nothing about her would be normal. Everything would be out of sync. She might as well accept that and deal with it.

Thirty minutes later, that task was also completed. By then neither had a clean or dry stitch on them. But Grace was thrilled that both gardens were back in perfect working order, only it was more obvious than ever how critically she needed to replenish the vegetables.

She voiced her thought. "I think I'll make a quick run to the nursery."

"I'll drive you," Denton said eagerly.

"That's not necessary."

He expelled a harsh breath. "How 'bout not arguing for once. Think that's possible?"

Curbing her anger at his high-handedness, she said, "I guess so."

His eyes twinkled. "Ah, we're making progress."

Grace realized she needed to lighten up, for her own sake if nothing else. After all, she'd let him stay, which meant she'd made the choice and had to pay the consequence. But she honestly hadn't known he would become her shadow. And while that was heady stuff, it was also dangerous. No way, she vowed again, could she let him back inside her heart.

"Why don't you drive my SUV?" she said.

"Come on, let's go."

Closed up in the vehicle with him, she became more aware of him than in the garden. Maybe it was the close confines. Or maybe she could better smell the distinctive odor of his cologne mixed with the sweat from his body. They made a potent cocktail.

She smothered a sigh and gritted her teeth. Get over it, she told herself. He would be leaving soon. This was all just a lark to him. When the pressure from Dallas become too great and he became too bored with all this "quaintness," he'd hit the road back to the city and not look back.

"Where is this place?" he asked.

His question jerked her out of her thoughts. "We're going to Mantooth nursery. It's been on Sycamore Street forever."

"A teacher and her husband owned it. Flora and Abe Mantooth, right?"

"Yep. She taught while her husband ran the nursery, only he's dead now."

"I had her for math."

"We all did."

"So she must be older than dirt."

Grace smiled. "Pretty close to it, I'm sure."

"You don't smile often enough," he said, cutting her a quick gaze. "Or is it just around me? After all, I barged in on you and messed up your playhouse."

"I don't think you want to go there."

He sighed. "No, I guess not. Anyway, here we are. I'd forgotten how easy it is to get around in a small town."

"Kind of nice, isn't it?" She stole a glance at him, a glance he unexpectedly returned. Their eyes held for a heartbeat.

"Yeah, it is," he said finally, an unreadable look in those green eyes.

"Ah, here comes Ms. Flora." Grace unbuckled her seat belt, breaking the tension. "She recognizes my vehicle."

"Regular customer, huh?"

"She needs the business."

They got out then and met the old woman halfway. Although she was almost painfully thin from hard work, and her face was severely wrinkled from years in the sun, her smile was bright and targeted on Grace.

"I was hoping you'd come today. I just got a shipment of new tomato plants."

"Oh, great." Grace turned to Denton, then back to Flora. "You recognize him?"

Flora peered hard at Denton, then chuckled. "Why you're Denton Hardesty, one of my most obnoxious students."

"That's right, ma'am," Denton drawled, extending a hand.

"Forget the handshake, boy," Flora said, "I want a hug."

Denton laughed good-naturedly as she gave him a bear hug before letting him go. "My, but it's good to see you. You were always a nice-looking boy, but you've made a downright handsome man."

"Why, thank you, ma'am," Denton drawled again, turning and winking at Grace.

That gesture sent her pulse skyrocketing. Careful, she warned herself afresh. You're letting his charm suck you in again. Remember he has no sticking power.

"So has business picked up any?" Grace asked in a rushed tone.

Denton cast her another look, but didn't say anything.

"No, it hasn't," Flora responded, her tone bleak. "But that new nursery out on the highway is mopping up."

"Maybe if you advertised," Grace suggested, angry that the people in town were deserting Flora.

"Can't afford it, honey. I'm doing good just to hang on." Suddenly her eyes filled with tears. "For Fred more than me. He would roll over in his grave, God rest his soul, if he thought I was thinking about closing this place."

"Is that what you want, Mrs. Mantooth?" Denton asked.

"Heavens, no. I love selling my plants and flowers.

Why, without any kids or close family, I don't know what I'd do. Grace knows what I mean, don't you, honey?''

"Unfortunately, I do, Flora," Grace said, feeling Denton's eyes on her at the same time her face suffused with color. She refused to look back at him for fear she'd see pity in his eyes—the last thing she wanted.

"I'd like to help," he said into the small silence.

Flora's jaw went slack. "You would?"

"Yes, ma'am."

"Pooh, son, stop that 'ma'am' stuff. I don't remember you being so polite when I was trying to teach you to add and subtract."

Denton's lips twitched and so did Grace's. Flora was in one of her salty moods today, which was good for both of them. Since Denton had strolled into the garden, he hadn't popped one antacid.

"All right, Flora, so the new kid on the block has come in and threatened your livelihood. Tell me what you need to keep up with the competition."

"Look around, sonny. There's not much I don't need."

Flora was right, Grace thought. The nursery was in a sad state. The greenhouses were practically falling down, and the plant and vegetable stands were so rickety they could topple at any moment. The building that served as an office and housed inside products was in even worse shape. It needed major repairs, especially the roof. When it rained, customers had to dodge buckets.

"So let me do some checking, and I'll get back to you," Denton said, rubbing his jaw while his gaze surveyed the premises.

Flora squinted her eyes at him. "Are you serious?"

"You bet."

"But you don't even live here anymore." She angled her head. "Why do you care?"

"I can't have anyone messing with my favorite teacher," Denton said lightly. "That's why."

"Hogwash," Flora said, though it was obvious she was pleased.

And relieved, Grace noted, watching as some of the years seemed to have dropped off her face, leaving her looking less weary and frightened. Bless Denton. This was a side of him she'd never seen, but then that wasn't surprising. Again, she'd known the boy not the man. Still, she'd never thought he'd be this thoughtful which proved how much a stranger he really was.

"Hogwash, huh?" Denton pitched his head back and laughed. "If we had said that in your class, we would've been sent to the office."

"But not before getting your mouth washed out with soap," Flora added with a grin.

"How old are you, Flora?" Denton asked.

"Eighty-one," she declared without offense.

"Damn," Denton muttered, turning to Grace. "They don't make 'em like her anymore."

"Oh, yes they do," Flora chimed in. "Grace'll be working until she drops."

"Flora!" Grace cried.

"Well, you will."

Denton laughed again which severed the good-natured argument.

"Look," Grace said, "I need to pick out my stuff and get back to the house. I have work to do."

Flora snorted but immediately began helping Grace

choose the very best variety of vegetables and plants. Once they were back in the SUV, Grace turned to Denton and said, "Thanks."

"For what?"

"You know. She's barely hanging on."

"That's obvious. I'll need you to put me in touch with some contractors and her banker so I can give her some operating money."

"I can't believe you're doing all this."

His gaze left the road and rested on her for a long second. "I've always had a secret passion to dig in the dirt, to work with plants, but there never seemed time for either. So..." He let his voice trail off.

"You just shoved that passion on the back burner," Grace said, finishing the sentence for him.

"That's the long and short of it."

"Maybe if you had indulged yourself, you wouldn't pop so many stomach pills."

"That's why I'm staying in Ruby."

She gave a start, dumbfounded that he admitted the fast track had gotten to him.

"Shocked, aren't you?" There was a teasing note in his voice.

"Yes," she said bluntly.

"So will you teach me how to relax?"

Loaded question. "Denton—"

"Forget I said that," he muttered gruffly.

He was turning into the drive, which saved her from having to respond. Maybe he'd leave her alone to finish her work in the garden. All this togetherness was beginning to get to her. Her body was a bundle of nerves.

No such luck. As before, he began working by her

side. Only after all the vegetable plants were in the ground did they stop.

"I appreciate all your help," she said at last, an uncertain note in her voice. On the one hand, she felt grateful; on the other, she felt annoyed. She hadn't wanted his help. She had wanted him to leave her alone.

Liar, a little voice taunted.

"I enjoyed the hell out of it," he responded. "Later I'll come back and work some more."

She decided not to argue, resigned to the fact that it was easier to give in than to fight him. On some things, that is, she corrected mentally. "Let's go in, and I'll pour us some tea."

They remained silent even after each had taken several sips out of glasses filled with apricot-flavored tea, her concoction, a specialty of the house.

"Man, this is good stuff."

"Thanks," she responded, that old suffocating feeling returning, especially since he had ambled around the bar and was now standing next to her.

"Know what?"

She swallowed, his husky-toned voice having drawn her eyes up to his. "What?"

"You have dirt on your lip."

Before she could say anything, he reached out and removed it with the tip of a finger.

"Don't," she whispered, a feeling of raw hunger surging through her. "That's becoming a habit."

"What?" he asked again, his tone having dropped to a huskier pitch.

"Touching...me."

Nine

"I...know," he whispered, his head inching lower. "Only, I can't stop myself."

"Denton..." Her voice was an aching plea, a plea for what she no longer knew. His nearness, his touch, were driving her wild.

"I love it when you say my name like that."

His lips were so close now she could feel his breath, taste his breath, *taste him*.

"We...shouldn't."

"Yes, we should."

She tried to turn her head, but his thumb, trailing a hot line across her trembling lower lip, prevented that move.

"Grace..."

It was her name, whispered with such agonized longing, that was her undoing, that made her throw caution to the wind and part her lips in anticipation.

He groaned, his hands digging savagely into her shoulders as he sank his mouth onto hers. Her breath caught in her throat as his lips seemed to sear hers with their heat while his tongue thrust its way inside and meshed with hers.

Her legs turned to water, and if he hadn't been holding on to her so tightly, they would've buckled under her.

He moaned, deepening the kiss at the same time he pressed the entire length of her lithe body into his. Instantly she felt his hardness stir against her lower abdomen, firing up the memory of that night long ago when nothing had been between them.

Only flesh against flesh.

She hadn't wanted this to happen, but now that he was ravishing her mouth, she was powerless to stop him, the heat from his lips, from his body, affecting every quivering nerve in hers.

She'd tried to tell herself that her mind could win over her body, that she was immune to him, but she knew now how wrong she'd been, how badly she had miscalculated. Both still remembered. Both still craved him, especially her *flesh*. How could that have happened? How could she have not seen this assault coming?

"Grace, Grace," he murmured, continuing to drain the sweet nectar from her lips.

She should be strong. She should stop him *now*. Instead, her breasts swelled, her nipples pebbled and her legs parted of their own violation to his seeking hand that had found its way there, probing, feeling, making her wet.

"I want you. Let's go to my room."

His gutturally spoken words were the catalyst that

brought her to her senses. With a superhuman effort, she jerked out of his arms. For a second thereafter they stared at each other, their breaths coming in gasps.

She had come so close...

Shivering uncontrollably, Grace wrapped her arms around herself and fought back the threat of tears. She wanted to disappear on the spot. Perhaps in another minute she would have capitulated, let him make love to her right here in the kitchen, writhing on the floor.

"Grace, it's okay," he said at last, though he didn't look or sound convinced of that. His voice had the rough edge of sandpaper. And he was pale, as if all the blood had been drained from his body.

"No, it's not," she said, fighting for a decent breath.

His gaze was intense. "I would never have done anything you didn't want to."

"I don't believe you."

"Yes, you do," he countered in a low, soft voice.

He was right. She knew he would never have forced himself on her. It was she who was the problem. In that moment of hot passion, she would've let him do anything he wanted and that was what galled her, what mortified her. But she couldn't tell him that. She had no intention of humiliating herself any further.

"Please, just leave me alone," she said, forcing her gaze off him and gnawing at her lower lip.

"You...we didn't do anything wrong, Grace. I wanted you and you wanted me. There's nothing wrong with that."

"You still don't get it, do you?" she retorted, widening her eyes.

"Oh, I get it, but I don't think you do."

"You haven't lost your ability to be a real jerk."

A pained expression darkened Denton's features. "I can't undo the past. If I could—"

"I have work to do." Her tone was pointed.

His mouth worked, and she knew he wanted to argue. But he didn't. Instead he pivoted on his heels and walked out of the kitchen. Within seconds she heard the front door open and close.

Good. He was gone. Permanently, she hoped, though she knew better. She wasn't about to get out of this mess so easily, not when the lust was still riding so close to the surface for both of them.

Somehow she managed to force herself to put one foot in front of the other, go to her quarters where she immediately shed her clothes and stepped into the shower, trying her best to wash Denton off her body and out of her thoughts.

Feeling tears sting her eyes, Grace leaned her head against the tile and let the warm water flow over her, along with uninvited memories.

After they had made love for the first time that wonderful spring afternoon, she'd been so sure Denton loved her and would forever, that they would end up marrying and living happily ever after.

Then the bottom had dropped out of her heart and her world. Two days later, he had told her his dad's transfer had gone through and his family was moving out of state. But even then she hadn't been all that disturbed, confident that no matter where he was he wouldn't forsake her, that as soon as he helped get his parents settled and himself back to school, he'd send for her.

After all, they had made love. She was his.

Still, she'd cried when he'd told her. He'd consoled her with hot, wet kisses.

"Don't, Grace," he'd begged, his lips all over her face. "I'll see you again soon."

"Do you promise?" she'd whispered, staring at him through worshipful eyes.

He'd grabbed her hand and placed it on his chest. "I promise."

That had never happened. After the move, his dad had had the stroke, and though they'd corresponded through letters and occasional phone calls, she'd never seen him again. Until he'd walked up on the porch of the B&B.

And she never knew why. And still didn't.

In light of that, how could she have dropped her guard and kissed him back with such wanton need, such careless abandonment? She felt so ashamed. But she had no one to blame but herself. She could've stopped him, and she hadn't.

He had to leave soon. He just had to.

Clinging to that thread of hope, Grace stepped out of the shower, dressed, then went back downstairs. Her part-time helper Connie Foley was in the foyer dusting.

She was thin and petite with a sweet spirit and sweet ways. Although she varied her days, she was a hard worker, and Grace couldn't run the B&B without her help, especially when it came to the cleaning.

"I noticed we have another guest," Connie said in her soft, shy tone. "That's wonderful. Now we're full again."

Unwittingly Grace frowned, then followed it with a forced smile. "He may be leaving anyday."

"Oh," Connie said, appearing confused.

Grace saw no reason to unconfuse her. At least for the remainder of the day, Denton was off-limits. She prayed he'd feel the same way about her and stay gone.

"I noticed all the work you did in the gardens."

"It took most of the morning, so I'm running behind."

"Where are Mr. and Mrs. Brenner?" Connie asked.

Grace was in the middle of explaining about Ed's attack when the front door opened and the Brenners walked in.

"Boy, am I glad to see you two," Grace cried, hugging them both.

Zelma winked at Connie. "Now all her chicks are back in place."

"That's right," Grace declared. "My guests are my family."

"I know, honey." Zelma smiled and hugged Grace again. "Believe me, we're glad to be back."

"Hospital food sucks," Ed muttered in a tone as dry as parchment.

The women laughed, then Grace accompanied Ed and Zelma to their room where she left Zelma fussing over her husband.

Thank goodness neither had asked about Denton, Grace thought as she made her way into the kitchen to prepare for snack time, praying again that she wouldn't have to deal with him.

Then it hit her about Flora. He couldn't leave until he made good on his promise to help her. Darn!

She had just finished filling the tray with cheese cubes, cucumber sandwiches and homemade sugar cookies when the phone rang.

"Why, hello, Roger," she said after the unfamiliar voice had identified itself.

Roger Gooseby was the local grocer and mayor, whom she didn't see all that often because Connie did most of the grocery shopping. He was a large, robust man whose heart was as big as his body. Everyone in Ruby thought highly of him and his wife.

"How are you?" Grace asked. "And Cynthia?"

"The wife's fine. Actually, we were all fine and dandy until yesterday."

"What happened?"

"Something terrible, or at least it has the potential."

Grace curbed her fear. "Oh, dear, what's wrong?"

"Ruby's being considered for a nuclear power plant."

Shock forced Grace to sit down. "No way!"

"That's how I feel and everyone else I've spoken to."

"So what do we do?" Grace asked in a crisp tone.

"Get organized and fight the bastards."

"I'll do my part. Just keep me posted."

"Will do."

Grace remained seated long after the conversation ended. A nuclear plant in Ruby? The far-reaching repercussions were too vast to comprehend, especially for her as the owner of a B&B. Her head fell into her hands, despair wreaking havoc inside her.

First Denton. Now this. What on earth was going to happen next to upend her life?

"Would you be opposed to an old lady kissing you?"

"Why, shucks, no," Denton drawled, his tone dripping with humor. "In fact, I can't think of anything else I'd like better." Except being with Grace, watching her at work in the house and garden, that sweet, contented smile lighting her face.

But since that wasn't going to happen, he'd settle for a peck on the cheek from Flora and be damn glad to get it.

When he'd stormed out of the house, he'd started driving, having no idea where he was going. It was only after he'd found himself in Austin that an idea hit him, thrusting him into action. He'd find a contractor himself who could hopefully begin work on the nursery repairs immediately. Within an hour he'd done just that.

He had just told Flora the good news. She giggled, sounding like a schoolgirl, though her voice cracked slightly from age.

"You're a good man, Denton Hardesty," she said, touching her dry lips to his cheek.

"Thank you, ma'am."

"So the worker comes tomorrow," Flora said in a tone filled with wonder.

"Workmen," Denton stressed. "There'll be a crew here, getting this place overhauled and quickly, too."

Flora blinked back tears. "I still can't believe it."

"We can't have those newcomers messing with you old-timers."

Flora swiped at a tear that got loose. "Where's Grace? You should've brought her with you."

He wished. "She's too busy to run the roads with me."

"If I were her age and unattached, I wouldn't be." Flora winked. "That's for sure. I'd be bound and determined to hogtie you, boy."

Denton laughed, and it felt good. "And right about now, I'd let you."

Following his bout with Grace, a dose of this crusty old lady was what his battered senses had needed. Along with a cold shower, he added cuttingly. Grace's rejection of him had smarted. Hell, who did she think she was kidding? She'd been as hot for him as he'd been for her. He hadn't forced her to kiss him; he hadn't forced her to do anything. She'd been hot and pliant, giving as good as she got and of her own free will.

It had been her free will that had called a halt. He should be glad. Making love to Grace no matter how badly he wanted would not have been wise. Too many complications. Too many strings.

No, she had done them both a favor. Now all he had to do was convince his body.

"Maybe one of these days if I live long enough, I'll be able to repay you," Flora said into the growing silence.

Denton snorted. "Forget that. Even if you made a million, I wouldn't take a penny of it. I'm doing this because I want to."

"Again, you're a good man, and you deserve a good woman."

"How 'bout you and me gettin' hitched?"

Flora slapped him on the shoulder. "Go on, get out of here. This old lady has work to do."

After he left the nursery, he drove around town, taking in all the changes that had come about since he'd left. Man, how this little place had grown, and all for the better, too. Too bad there was nothing here for him.

Grace.

He gripped the steering wheel until his knuckles whitened. She was there all right, only not for him. He'd had his chance and squandered it. That road was now closed, which was best for both of them. Were it not for the aching hole left inside him from unquenched desire, he might have reconciled that within himself. But for now he couldn't.

If he had any sense, he'd do himself and Grace a favor. He would keep on driving until he reached Dallas, his home, where he belonged. For the most part this town, these people, were foreign to him. He no longer had anything in common with any of them nor did he want to.

His life, his needs were in the city.

Suddenly he found himself at the highway intersection. He didn't so much as hesitate. He turned and headed back to the B&B, back to Grace.

Ten

Grace moved like a robot on automatic pilot during the remainder of the afternoon, the mayor's disturbing call returning to mind. In fact, she worked herself into such a state she took time and made several calls to other B&B owners. Some had heard the news and others hadn't. But all were equally concerned and ready to band together to fight. The organizational part she was still leaving to Roger Gooseby, though she would do her part.

She feared for her business if Ruby was chosen. The other owners felt the same way. If she lost her livelihood, she would have no recourse but to return... No! She shut her mind to that thought, feeling panic well inside her. Ruby wouldn't be chosen. It simply wouldn't.

Now, at the moment, she was once again obsessing on Denton. He hadn't made an appearance during snack time or since, which was fine by her. Yet she found herself unconsciously flinching, then peering over her shoulder, every time a door opened and closed.

She figured she had so much to do—from replacing the wallpaper in her bath upstairs, to catching up on her book work, to planning the rest of the week's breakfast and snack menus, that she wouldn't have time to think about him.

Wrong.

Both her thoughts and heart continued to dwell on him, especially that lethal kiss. Even though she'd already beaten up on herself for her part in it, she truly hadn't wanted it to end. All the emotion, all the love she had felt for him was back, and her heart felt shattered all over again.

Surely she wasn't still in love with him. Unwilling to probe such a provocative thought, Grace tore out of the kitchen and made her way outside. Once there, she took several deep, gulping breaths, then felt the world suddenly right itself. The thought of being closed up was too much for her. She needed air and space.

Maybe she'd gotten her wish after all, she told herself, continuing to fight off the building sense of desperation. Maybe he'd already left.

Maybe the kiss had scared the living daylights out of him and he was halfway back to Dallas. For a second her world brightened. Then her sound judgment kicked in and warned her not to hold her breath. Anyway, she couldn't run from the emotions he stirred in her. She'd already tried to once and it hadn't worked. She had to face them, then defeat them, or she'd be lost.

But dammit, that wasn't fair. He'd broken her soul into little pieces and gotten away with it. No one should have to endure a second round of abuse. The answer was strength and resolve. She could and would pull herself back together one more time.

As soon as he left.

Holding her shoulders back, Grace made her way into the metal building where she stored her garden supplies. Shortly she was in the front yard, on her knees yanking out weeds. Maintaining her precious flower beds could be an everyday, all-consuming chore if she let it. Today, though, it was the panacea for her battered senses, and she welcomed the challenge.

"Hey, want some help?"

Grace looked up and Zelma was on the front porch, glass of iced tea in hand.

"No, thanks. You take care of Ed."

She made a face, then grinned. "That old coot. He's one for the books. He's in there holding court, ordering me around like you wouldn't believe."

"And you love every minute of it."

This time Zelma's grin was sheepish. "You're right, I do. I'm just glad he's going to be all right."

"Isn't that the truth," Grace said, wiping perspiration off her brow.

Zelma frowned. "Why don't you let Connie do that?"

"Because she has too much to do inside."

"I could help out on both counts."

"Not on your life. You're a guest, for heaven's sake. I'm supposed to take care of you."

"That's baloney. I'm used to working like a field hand."

"Well, not anymore. Ed's seeing to that. Now, you just relax and enjoy."

"All right. I'll take the old coot for a walk out back, then we'll rest in the swing for a while."

Grace grinned, wiping her face again. "Sounds like a good plan. I'll see you later." She paused. "I have something I want to discuss with you and Ed."

"What's wrong with now?"

"I'd prefer later." They were such a sound, responsible couple she wanted to get their take on what might happen concerning the nuclear plant threat, but not until she had her scattered emotions under wraps. Right now, she didn't.

If things had been different, she would have loved to get Denton's opinion on the matter. With his connections, he might even be able to help derail things. But that would be a dangerous move. She didn't want to involve him in town politics or anything else that was personal.

Forget him.

"Later it is," Zelma quipped, turning and going back inside.

Grace sat back on the grass for a minute, thinking she ought to go inside and get herself something to drink. Zelma would've brought her some tea had she asked. Ah, forget it, she told herself. It was getting late, and she should finish this flower bed, wind up this project for the day. She dreaded the evening, dreaded it stretching in front of her, long and lonely.

It was his fault.

If he hadn't come back to Ruby and turned her life upside down, her insides wouldn't be so mangled. It was in that moment that she heard the vehicle. Her heart faltered. He had come back. Both excitement and dread held her motionless until she felt his presence behind her.

"Something tells me we've been bitten by the same bug."

That low, husky voice that she'd come to associate exclusively with him further assaulted her already-raw nerves.

She scrambled to her feet. No way was she going to carry on a conversation with him sitting down. Although she wasn't nearly his height, standing up seemed somehow to even the odds, at least in her mind.

"And what bug would that be?" she said, trying to keep the tremor out of her voice. But it was hard, as he had a certain look in his eyes, a vulnerable look, as though he didn't know quite what to do next. If she was right about that, then that was probably a first with him. He usually oozed self-confidence.

"Work," he murmured, his eyes raking over her, seeming to concentrate on the vee of her shirt where she had a gathering of perspiration. "That's all you seem happy doing."

Color crept into her face. She couldn't even be around him without being aware of strong, sexual vibes. She didn't know how much longer she could play this cat and mouse game and endure.

"I guess you should know," she said lamely, trying not to stare at him.

"Do I still have my room?"

Their eyes met for another quick moment, then both turned away as if they'd been zapped.

Grace tried to find enough breath to speak again, but it was difficult. Now was her chance to tell him no, tell him he was no longer welcome, tell him whatever it would take to get rid of him.

"That's…up to you," she said. So much for the mental lecture.

"I'd like to stay."

"Denton—"

"How 'bout going on the porch?" He peered down, then back up. "If you're not through here, I can finish up later."

While she had no intention of letting him finish weeding the front beds, she didn't say that. Actually, the thought of just talking to him as if everything was normal as apple pie and ice cream left a bad taste in her mouth. Yet she couldn't let him know how she felt, how attracted she was to him, how *frightened* she was of that attraction.

Perhaps it was a thread of desperation she heard in his tone that made her turn and head toward the swing, then perch on one end of it. Thankfully, he chose the wicker chair next to her.

"I wouldn't blame you if you kicked me out."

Color rushed into her cheeks, knowing he was referring to the kiss. "That subject's off-limits."

"Would an apology help?"

"No."

"Didn't think so." He trapped her gaze. "I wasn't going to apologize, anyway, because I'm not sorry."

The intensity of his eyes seemed to literally burn her skin, deepening her color. "It's no big deal," she lied. "Just don't do it again."

He didn't respond for what seemed the longest time, then he said, "I've been at the nursery."

"Flora's?" she asked inanely.

"Yep, but not before driving to Austin."

The Silhouette Reader Service™ — Here's how it works:

Accepting your 2 free books and gift places you under no obligation to buy anything. You may keep the books and gift and return the shipping statement marked "cancel." If you do not cancel, about a month later we'll send you 6 additional novels and bill you just $3.34 each in the U.S., or $3.74 each in Canada, plus 25¢ shipping & handling per book and applicable taxes if any.* That's the complete price and — compared to cover prices of $3.99 each in the U.S. and $4.50 each in Canada — it's quite a bargain! You may cancel at any time, but if you choose to continue, every month we'll send you 6 more books, which you may either purchase at the discount price or return to us and cancel your subscription.

*Terms and prices subject to change without notice. Sales tax applicable in N.Y. Canadian residents will be charged applicable provincial taxes and GST.

If offer card is missing write to: Silhouette Reader Service, 3010 Walden Ave., P.O. Box 1867, Buffalo NY 14240-1867

NO POSTAGE
NECESSARY
IF MAILED
IN THE
UNITED STATES

BUSINESS REPLY MAIL

FIRST-CLASS MAIL   PERMIT NO. 717-003   BUFFALO, NY

POSTAGE WILL BE PAID BY ADDRESSEE

SILHOUETTE READER SERVICE
3010 WALDEN AVE
PO BOX 1867
BUFFALO NY 14240-9952

Play The Lucky Hearts Game

and get...
FREE BOOKS & a FREE GIFT...
YOURS to KEEP!

Yes! I have scratched off the silver card. Please send me my **2 FREE BOOKS** and **FREE MYSTERY GIFT**. I understand that I am under no obligation to purchase any books as explained on the back of this card.

Scratch Here!
then look below to see what your cards get you.

326 SDL DC56   **225 SDL DC5Z**

NAME   (PLEASE PRINT CLEARLY)

ADDRESS

APT.#   CITY

STATE / PROV.   ZIP/POSTAL CODE

Twenty-one gets you
2 FREE BOOKS and a
FREE MYSTERY GIFT!

Twenty gets you
2 FREE BOOKS!

Nineteen gets you
1 FREE BOOK!

TRY AGAIN!

Visit us online at
www.eHarlequin.com

Offer limited to one per household and not valid to current Silhouette Desire® subscribers. All orders subject to approval.

She frowned. "I'm not following you."

He smiled briefly then explained.

"You mean it was that simple?" Her tone sounded dazed even to her own ears.

"Only if it all comes together. We'll see."

"I'm impressed and elated."

"I was hoping you would be."

Grace didn't dare probe that declaration for fear of sinking a little deeper into the surrounding quagmire. "I hope it isn't all for naught."

"What does that mean?" he demanded, narrowing his eyes and rubbing his slightly bristled chin.

She told him about her conversation with the mayor.

Denton let go of an expletive. "That's gotta be nixed."

"We all feel that way, but you know the kind of ammo it takes to fight that kind of thing."

"Do you mind if I do some poking, see what I can do?"

"Why would you do that?" she asked, voicing her skepticism.

"I think you know why," he said huskily, his eyes once again deep and searching. "For you."

Grace lunged to her feet, both her body and her voice quivering, "Stop it, damn you."

Before he could mount a suitable defense, she darted inside and slammed the door behind her.

She hated crying.

More than that, she hated feeling that awful sense of impending doom hovering over her like a dark cloud. She had tried to sleep, but couldn't. So instead of continuing to fight the bed, especially the pillow, she got up and made her way downstairs in the wee hours of the morning, hoping a glass of hot milk would stave off an attack.

She had just taken her cup out of the microwave when her hand began to shake, slopping the liquid all over the floor. But the mess was the least of her worries as her heart began to race off the charts, her breathing became labored, and her head spun.

She was having a full-blown anxiety attack, something she hadn't had in a long time. Giving in to the tears that ran down her face, she groped for the cabinet where she kept spare medication. Once she'd swallowed a tiny pill, she clung to the counter and waited for the room to settle.

"Grace, what the hell?"

Oh, dear Lord, not him, not the reason for her attack in flesh and blood.

"Go away, Denton," she whispered, between sobs. "You seem to have a talent for showing up at the wrong place."

"And at the wrong time," he added in a defeated voice.

"That's…right," she whispered, beginning to shake again.

"Grace, let me help," he pleaded. "You're ill. Even I can see that."

"No!" she cried. "I'm having an anxiety attack." Rarely did she share that secret with anyone. In fact, she kept it closely guarded, hating that weakness in herself. That was why she couldn't believe she'd just blurted it out, to him of all people, especially since she blamed him for bringing it on.

Denton suddenly closed the distance between them, and before she could get out of harm's way, he placed his hands on her forearms and drew her gently against him.

"Please, let me hold you," he said in a thick, tortured voice.

Heaven on earth was the thought that went through her mind. For the first time since the attack had rendered her useless, she felt safe, cocooned in a secure warmth that only his arms could provide.

Fool! she lambasted herself.

"Grace, Grace," he whispered, "I'm so sorry." He then ran a soothing hand up and down her back.

She couldn't speak; all she could do was cling to him.

Eleven

He knew he should push her away, that it was the sensible, logical thing for both of them. But how could he let her go when she was holding on to him for dear life? He didn't kid himself, though. Right now she was frightened, for some unknown reason, and he was her comforter. No way would he take advantage of her pain. Lord knows, he'd been down that same road with the plane crash.

Still, just having her in his arms and holding her was ripping his guts to pieces. He wanted more, so much more. He wanted to kiss her lips, suckle her breasts, lick her flesh all the way down to her toes.

Those erotic thoughts hardened him instantly, and he knew she felt him pressing against her. But that was the way it was between them, the way it had always been. When they touched, it was like a lethal combustion. Time or distance had not changed that.

All he could do now was hope he had the restraint to conquer his growing desire and not do anything else he would be sorry for.

"Shh," he whispered into her sweet-smelling hair. "It's going to be all right. You're going to be all right."

"No, I'm not." Her cry was muffled against his chest where he felt her tears soak his shirt.

"Yes, you are. Trust me on that."

She pulled back then and peered into his eyes. "I hate it when this happens."

"I'm sure," he said in a soothing voice, pulling her next to him again, only this time he couldn't stop himself from dropping featherlight kisses on her temple, then her cheeks, tasting her tears, *tasting her.*

A tiny sigh escaped her as he lifted her wide, tear-lined eyes to his, her lower lips trembling slightly. That was his undoing. With a groan he lowered his lips to hers, gently at first, then, when she didn't object, he deepened the pressure, becoming hard and hungry.

She moaned against him but still offered no objection, not even when his hand found its way to a burgeoning breast. He pulled on the nipple, feeling it bud under his fingers like a flower bursting to bloom.

"Grace," he whispered against her soft, moist lips. "I want you so much."

"Then…make love to me."

Denton pulled back and stared at her, unable to believe those broken words had come from her. But when she reached up and traced a finger over his lips, lingering on the moist inside of his bottom one, he knew she was serious.

Though his legs had all the consistency of water,

he forced them to move, with her adhered to his side. No words were exchanged, not even after they reached his room, where clothes were instantly discarded and they lay naked on the huge bed.

"Tell me what you want," he rasped, his gaze soaking up the beauty of her creamy-skinned body that still had all the curves in the right places.

"You. All of you."

He needed no second invitation, leaning over and taking her mouth once again in deep, hot kisses, tongues toying, then sparring. Fearing that he couldn't hold off much longer, but wanting to savor all of her, he pulled away and moved to her nipples where he pulled and tugged with his mouth until they were swollen and pulsating.

"Oh, Denton," she whispered, running her hands wildly through his hair before slowly making her way down his stomach to the crisp curls between his thighs. Velvet-like fingers surrounded his manhood, then moved up and down.

He moaned against the raw heat that shot through his body even as his tongue dipped in and out of her navel, further sparking the fire inside him to a feverish pitch. Still, he wanted to prolong the sweet misery, make this moment last forever.

It was then that his hand nudged her thighs apart and his tongue speared into her quivering moistness. Her hips bucked, and moans of pleasure erupted from her lips before he raised himself over her.

"Please, don't torture me anymore," she pleaded, reaching for him.

He thrust into her ever so slowly, his eyes glued to hers, watching the play of emotions across her face as he continued to move in, then out, extending the exquisite pain.

"Denton, please!" she cried.

This time he remained inside her, thrusting hard and high until they both cried out in unison and he collapsed on top of her.

"My sweet, sweet Grace," he murmured against her breasts.

Denton watched her for the longest time, determined to memorize every detail of her face and body, store it in his heart so that when he no longer had access to her he could draw on his vivid memory.

He stifled a groan, aching to touch a breast that was exposed to his greedy gaze. The streetlamp shone through the gauzy drapes and bathed her in a misty glow, allowing him that pleasure.

How could he walk away and leave her again? It would be even harder this time. But what choice did he have? None. His life was miles away from here. This time the groan escaped, and her eyes opened.

At first she seemed confused, then shocked at seeing him bending over her, watching her. Then she smiled, the most beautiful smile he'd ever seen.

"Thank you," she whispered.

He could barely talk around the lump in his throat. "For what?"

"For saving my life."

"I hardly think I did that." His voice was far from back to normal. He sounded as if he'd swallowed a rusty nail.

"Yes, you did. When I have one of my...attacks, I always feel like I'm dying."

"Oh, Grace, how long have you had those things?"

"Too long."

"Is that why you've been content and secure to stay here in quiet and peaceful Ruby?"

"That's part of the reason, but I also love it here. It's home."

Home. Did he have a home? Somehow he didn't think so. Suddenly that thought was unsettling. Even when he'd been married, he'd never really come home.

Denton crooked his elbow and stared directly into her eyes. "What triggers those awful attacks?" he asked, wanting to know everything about her, yet knowing he had no right. "Was it—" He broke off unable to find the right words to ask the deadly question that festered in his mind.

"You leaving me," she said, finishing the sentence for him.

He nodded on a deep sigh.

"No. They started much later." She turned away.

"Grace?"

She faced him again, but her eyes were shuttered. He had run into a brick wall. He knew there was more, but she had said all she intended to say on the subject. He had no choice but to respect that. He'd given up the right to pry long ago.

"For the most part, I'm okay," she said. "I have medication that usually kills them on target."

Her word choice made him smile. "That's good."

She stretched suddenly, and when she did her leg brushed against him. He got an instant response.

Her eyes widened. "Oh, dear."

He chuckled, then sobered. "See what you do to me, woman."

"That works both ways." Grace's tone faltered.

"So are you telling me you're wet?" he whispered, his eyes darkening.

"Yes," she said sweetly and simply.

The room was quiet for a long time.

Once they were sated again, Grace eased out of the bed and went into the bathroom. There she leaned over the counter and clung to it, deciding that she had indeed lost her sanity.

Lifting her head, she stared at herself in the mirror, wondering if she looked any different after having made love following such a long abstinence? No. In fact, there was a glow about her that said she'd been made love to countless times.

Regrets?

Did she have any? No. At least not now. As for the "later" of all this, she wouldn't deal with that now. She intended to block out the coming of dawn and with it the reality of the new day. At present she was enjoying a moment of heaven on earth, and she had every intention of wallowing in it.

"What took you so long?" he asked, a lazy smile on his lips.

She chuckled. "None of your business."

"I missed you."

"I'm...glad."

"Grace—"

Her name sounded like a cry, and the look on his face was tormented. She knew what was coming—*his regrets*. And she didn't want to hear then, not now, not ever.

"It's your turn," she said quickly, climbing back onto the bed.

"For what?"

"To share your secrets."

"What makes you think I have any?"

"Intuition."

"Mmm."

She poked him in the ribs. "Come on, confess."

"What makes you think there's anything?"

"Woman's intuition."

He snorted.

"Come on, confess. Something makes you pop antacids. And I'll bet it's not all your job."

Denton sighed deeply. "You're right, it's not. It's been almost a year now, but I was involved in a plane crash."

"Oh, my God, Denton, I had no idea."

"There's no reason you would. It was in the Dallas paper, but that's all, as far as I know."

When she didn't respond, he went on, "I walked away with barely a scratch, but I was the only one."

"That's unbelievable," she said, an obvious hitch in her voice.

"I know. There were three of us in a private jet, out for fun on a spring day."

She picked up on the pain in his voice and was glad he didn't try to mask it. Maybe talking about it would help purge some of the pain that had apparently been festering for so long.

"My best friend had just bought the small jet. He hired a pilot and away we went. We'd been in the air quite a while when something went terribly wrong." He paused, his lips thinning.

She clasped his hand in hers and squeezed it. "Go on."

"I don't remember a lot of the details. Maybe I've just blotted them out. Who the hell knows? The shrinks don't, that's for sure. Anyway, the plane lost power and down we went. My friend, who was sitting next to the pilot, died on impact. I was in the back. That may be why I survived. Again, who the hell knows?''

"It's hard to ever get over that trauma no matter how long you live,'' Grace said gently, nestling closer to him.

"I'm finding that out. Guilt eats at my gut constantly, and it's been hard to get my life back on track. Actually, I haven't,'' he added bluntly.

"It takes more time for some than others.''

"It's just since I've been in Ruby that I realized how exhausted and burned-out I am.''

It was on the tip of her tongue to tell him he was welcome to stay in town, that he was welcome in her bed, in her life. And while he was definitely confused for the moment, it wouldn't last. Asking him to stay here with her would be the same as trapping, then caging, a wild creature.

"I haven't popped an antacid in hours now,'' he commented, interrupting her thoughts.

"You really ought to throw those things away for good.''

"Maybe I can. Now.''

His gaze made another disturbing sweep of her naked flesh.

"We'll work on that,'' she said, her pulse rate zooming again.

"It wasn't burnout alone that kept me here.''

Grace didn't know where he was going with that heavily loaded statement, and she wasn't sure she wanted to know. She had sworn he would never have the chance to hurt her again. By allowing him carte blanche over her body, she had done just that. However, she was going to stick to her resolve and not dwell on or repent of that sin now. Dawn would come soon enough.

"I never forgot you, you know," he admitted into the silence.

"I find that hard to believe," she countered uneasily.

"That's understandable. I acted like an ass."

"I won't argue that point," she said in a dull tone.

"But I was scared, especially after I found out you were a virgin."

"That was no excuse."

"I know, but—"

"I wasn't going to force you to marry me," she responded in a bleak tone. "You should've known that."

"I did know, but I just lost it. I was too immature to handle a serious relationship. Ugly as it is, that's the truth."

She wished now she hadn't opened this can of worms. Rehashing the past was much more painful than she'd anticipated. But maybe it was something that needed to be done so that she could lay it to rest once and for all. She likened it to Denton talking about the crash.

"And I'll admit my parents didn't help," he went on. "When Dad told me he was being transferred and that I was expected to move with them, I felt almost relieved. Then he had the stroke…"

"They manipulated you, Denton, especially after they found out about us."

"You're right. They did. I could see that later. At the time I couldn't." He paused and drew a shuddering breath. "Then I did another stupid thing. I married a woman I didn't love and thought it would work."

"What do you want me to say, Denton, that I forgive you?"

"Do you?" he asked huskily.

Yes, she said silently, because I never stopped loving you. But she couldn't tell him that. Loving him was her problem, not his.

"Is my forgiveness important to you?"

"God, yes."

"Then you have it," she said in a small voice.

He stared at her through unreadable eyes, then he grabbed her and pulled her on top of him.

"Make love to me again," he whispered in a frantic tone.

Twelve

"**I** believe that was the best ever, honey."

Ed was referring to the breakfast they had all scarfed down, leaving nothing to put in the disposal.

Although Grace flushed with pleasure, she made an embarrassed gesture with a hand. "You say that every time, Ed."

"Well, I happen to agree with him," Ralph added in his low, easy voice.

Grace's eyes widened, and Zelma actually chuckled out loud.

"See," Ed said in a know-it-all tone.

"It was just bacon and eggs, for heaven's sake."

"Oh, for heaven's sake," Zelma mimicked, "it was much more than that. The grits casserole and fried green tomatoes were out of this world."

"Don't forget the homemade croissants," Ralph chimed in.

"Well, thanks, guys," Grace said, her face redder than ever.

Zelma cocked her head to one side. "To what do we owe this occasion?"

For a second Grace was tempted to ignore Zelma's direct question for fear of giving herself away, of blurting out the truth about her happy frame of mind, how she'd been hoping to impress Denton with her culinary skills.

Only he hadn't even shown up for the feast.

"I just felt like going all out," Grace said in as nonchalant and light a tone as she could muster. In reality her heart felt frozen inside her chest. Where was he?

"And the fact that we ate on the back veranda made the feast even nicer," Ed said, breaking into her thoughts before crossing to the sink, where Grace stood, and giving her a peck on the cheek. "Don't let my wife give you a hard time, honey. I don't have to have a reason. I just love being pampered, and I definitely feel that." He winked at Grace, making her laugh.

"Hey, you old coot, you stop flirting now, you hear?" Zelma demanded, a hint of laughter in her voice. "She'll have you so spoiled when we get home, I won't know what to do with you."

"Then don't go," Grace said off the top of her head.

Zelma appeared taken aback for a second, then said, "While that sounds tempting, my kids and his have other ideas."

"I know," Grace said. "It's just you can't blame me for trying. I'm going to miss you two something awful when you leave."

Ralph chose that moment to shove back his chair and stand. "Er...thanks again. I've got to get back to the salt mines."

"I'm going to miss you, too, Ralph," Grace said softly, giving him a sweet smile.

Seemingly embarrassed, he shuffled his feet before giving her a faint smile and walking out.

"What a strange man," Zelma said, shaking her head.

"Now, Z," Ed said in a loving but chastising voice, "he just does his own thing. Nothing wrong with that."

"Believe it or not, he writes some of the funniest and most adoring children's stories you'd ever want to read," Grace added. "He's given me several to read."

Zelma shook her head in wonder. "I choose not to believe it, but if you say so..." Her voice trailed off.

"You reckon he'll autograph a couple for our grandkids?" Ed asked, scratching his head.

"Ask him," Grace said.

Zelma rolled he eyes. "Not me."

Grace chuckled. "Then I will."

"By the way, where's the hunk?" Zelma asked unexpectedly. "I can't believe he missed this treat."

"I haven't the foggiest," Grace said in what she hoped was an even tone, though she turned away from their inquiring eyes just in case she hadn't pulled it off.

"Come to think about it," Zelma said, "I saw him leave as I was heading for the kitchen."

In spite of herself, Grace felt her heart falter. "Leave?"

"He had his keys in hand," Zelma responded with

a shrug. "I'll have to make it a point to tell him what he missed."

"I doubt he cares," Grace said before she thought.

Zelma's eyebrows lifted. "I detect a note of sarcasm hidden in those words."

"Now, Z, leave the child alone." Ed grinned at Grace. "She's famous for her matchmaking skills."

Grace forced a smile. "Well, she's wasting her time with me, Ed. Anyway, Denton's just passing through."

"Sounds to me like he's not passing anywhere, that he's pretty stationary."

"Zelma, honey, you're wasting your time," Grace said, forcing another smile. "Now you two get out of here, and let me get this mess cleaned up."

"All right, my friend," Zelma said, "we'll see you at snack time, if we're back, that is. We're going into Austin to shop."

Grace frowned. "Are you up to that, Ed?"

"You betcha. I'm feeling no pain."

"Trust me, the old coot is as full of piss and vinegar as he ever was."

This time Grace's smile was genuine. "You two are a piece of work."

A few minutes later she was alone with nothing but her torrid thoughts. Although she felt none of the regrets that she'd felt certain would hit her this morning, she did feel a keen sense of disappointment that she hadn't seen him. Was *he* sorry? Perhaps. Or just reluctant to face her for whatever reason—for many reasons? Suddenly battling a feeling of nausea, Grace placed a hand over her lower stomach and took several deep breaths. Momentarily she felt a little better.

Maybe he was upset with her because she hadn't

awakened him before she'd left, just as dawn was breaking. But he'd been sleeping so soundly, like a satisfied baby who had his tummy full. Well, Denton had been satisfied, all right, but not with food. Their marathon sex had done the trick. Too, she hadn't known what to say. Asking him to stay was out of the question. Asking when he planned to leave was also out of the question.

Both required nerve, a special kind of nerve that she hadn't developed. Oh, her skin had definitely thickened, but not to that extent. Who was she kidding? When it came to Denton nothing had changed; he had the same kind of power over her that he'd had years ago.

What did that say about her?

She still loved him and wanted to be with him the rest of her life. Not going to happen, she told herself. Or was it possible, after all? She sensed he cared deeply for her. Or was she wrong and their relationship was based on sex like it had been years ago? Although at the time she'd thought it had been much more.

Picking up a dish towel, Grace began wiping the cabinet until there wasn't a spot on it. Yet she kept on rubbing, wondering if he'd taken the easy way out again, or rather the chicken way, and left.

If so, fine.

Her lips tightened into a white line. If he wanted to pretend last night hadn't happened, then she could oblige him without a problem. Over the years she had become quite adept at hiding her emotions, especially after she'd been diagnosed with anxiety attacks. She could be just as blasé about their lovemaking as he could.

She could do no such thing, she told herself savagely, not when her heart was breaking all over again. Last night had rekindled so many heated memories she'd thought she had laid to rest in the secret part of her soul, that she was a basket case this morning.

Only because he'd left without reassuring her that last night had meant as much to him as it had to her. But she knew in the light of day that great sex was all they would ever have going for them, that a future was impossible.

She had no intention of leaving Ruby, and he had no intention of staying here. Give it a rest, Grace told herself, slapping the towel down on the cabinet. She could wrestle this demon the rest of her life and never conquer it.

All she had to do now was simply get through the time he remained, then begin to glue the broken parts of her heart and soul back together one more time.

Deciding to cut some fresh flowers for Connie to place in each of the rooms, Grace grabbed the scissors out of the drawer and headed toward the French doors that led onto the veranda.

She had just placed her hand on the knob when the phone rang. "Darn," she muttered, not wanting to be trapped inside for a moment longer. Fresh air was what she most needed to help soothe her troubled mind.

Still, the phone was linked to her livelihood and she couldn't just not answer it. Crossing the room, she reached for the receiver.

It was Ward Pearson, a local rancher, the only man she'd gone out with since returning to Ruby. Although she cared deeply about Ward, she wasn't attracted to him and never had been. He was a widower with grown children, and while he hadn't been pushy in his efforts to woo her, Grace knew that if she gave the slightest indication that she would marry him, he'd take her up on it in a blink.

Not going to happen, especially now, not after Denton had breezed back into her life and proved anew that marrying Ward would definitely be settling for second best.

"Hello, Ward," she finally said, following his friendly greeting. "Long time no hear from."

"I've been out of town. One of the girls had surgery."

"Is everything okay?"

"Jim Dandy," he responded. "So what's going on with you?"

"You haven't heard," Grace said flatly.

He seemed to have picked up on that certain vibe in her tone because he responded accordingly. "What's wrong?"

"Well, Roger's much more in the know than me, but I can at least clue you in." She went on to explain about the nuclear plant site and how everyone felt.

"That's not going to happen as long as I'm breathing," he said in a low, terse tone. "No one's going to put a blight on this town when there are worlds of other sites that will work."

"You need to call Roger."

"I have a ton of messages, but I haven't listened to any of them yet. I'm sure he's one of them."

"I'd say he's probably more than one."

Ward chuckled in his low, gruff voice. "When can I see you?"

"Oh, Ward, I don't know."

"That seems to be your pat answer."

Grace felt a flush come over her face and was glad he couldn't see it. Guilt. That was what she was feeling right now and didn't know why. It was okay if she didn't want to go out with him, *sleep* with him. She was an adult and accountable to no one.

Except Denton, and only in her heart.

"It's not a good time. I have a full house, and you know how hectic that can be."

His deep sigh filtered through the line. "What if I won't take no for an answer?"

Although he spoke lightly, she knew he wasn't teasing. "I guess I'd be flattered."

"I just want to take you to dinner. Just think about it. Don't say no. Okay?"

"All right, Ward, I'll give your dinner invitation serious thought, although it might not be until next week."

"I can live with that. So I'll talk to you later, and don't worry about that plant. It's not going to happen."

"You have no idea how much better that makes me feel."

"Take care."

"Thanks, Ward."

She had just replaced the phone when she heard a sound behind her. Whirling around, she saw Denton standing in the doorway of the kitchen, his face devoid of color. She placed a hand over her chest, fear clutching at her. Had something happened? Other than his lack of color, nothing else seemed amiss. As usual, he looked as sexy as hell, even more so when visions of their erotic night flashed before her eyes.

He had on a pair of shorts and a T-shirt, as if he was about to hit the jogging trail. Maybe that was where he'd gone, only to correct that thought instantly as there wasn't one drop of sweat on him.

"Who was that on the phone?" he asked.

His blunt question took her so aback that for a moment she couldn't respond. Then when she did, she answered with a question, "Why do you ask?"

"I heard you mention the name Ward, then something about going out with him."

She was more than taken aback now; she was flabbergasted. "Were you eavesdropping on my conversation?"

"No, but I couldn't help but overhear."

Was he jealous? Was that what this was all about? For a moment her pulse leaped. "Actually, I was speaking to Ward Pearson, who's a friend."

"Are you two having an affair?"

She gasped, and her eyes widened. "Why...why would you ask such a thing?"

Silence fell over the room like a wet blanket.

"Because he's the client I'm here to see."

Thirteen

Money.

So that was what this was all about. Damn him! Grace warded off the sudden threat of tears and jutted out her chin. Jealous. Hysterical laughter almost erupted before she caught her lower lip between her teeth and bit down on it.

"I know what you're thinking—" Denton broke off as if searching for the words that would get him out of hot water.

"No, I don't think you do," she retorted, "or you wouldn't have said that."

It was obvious from the contrite look on his face that he wished he could recall his words and start over, but it was too late. As far as she was concerned, the damage had been done.

Last night had meant nothing to him. His career was heads above everything else.

"Tell me something, Denton, is the almighty dollar that important to you?"

This time his features darkened. "Dammit, Grace, if you'd just let me explain."

She stood her ground. "I asked you a simple question."

"No, it isn't," he responded through clenched teeth.

"Sure."

Her blatant sarcasm brought a flush to his face. "I knew you wouldn't believe me. That's why I wanted to explain."

"There are not enough words in the English language that would allow you to do that."

He muttered a curse just as Zelma rounded the corner. "Oh, I'm sorry," she said, halting midstride. "Sorry, I didn't mean to interrupt."

"I thought you two were going to Austin," Grace said.

"Me, too," Zelma replied, slightly down in the mouth. "But things didn't work out that way."

If the situation hadn't been so volatile, and her heart hadn't been hanging in shreds, she wouldn't have laughed at the picture Zelma made. For some reason her hair was all askew on her head. And her eyes were wide and smudged with makeup. She looked like someone out of a circus. And totally frayed.

"Sure I'm not interrupting?" Zelma's tone was as doubtful as her features.

"I'm sure," Grace said, dragging a deep breath through her lungs.

Zelma glanced from one to the other, then added

bluntly, ''Well, you two look as if you're about ready to blow a gasket.''

Leave it to Zelma to cut straight to the heart of the matter, Grace thought, hiding a smile.

Denton did chuckle, which definitely helped defuse the tension.

''I think that's a pretty apt term,'' he said, though the humor didn't seem to reach his eyes.

''Oh, dear,'' Zelma murmured meekly, resting her gaze on Grace.

''Don't pay any attention to him,'' Grace snapped. ''What did you need?''

Zelma waved a hand. ''Forget it. It's nothing that can't wait.''

''Our discussion is what can wait,'' Grace said, hoping that Denton would take the hint and disappear. Despite the fact that she still loved him, she couldn't bear the sight of him, not right now, anyway.

Zelma frowned. ''Oh, I don't—''

''Zelma!''

''Okay, okay. It's Ed.''

''What about him?'' Denton asked quickly.

Grace battled down her fear. ''Is it his heart?''

''No, no, nothing like that,'' Zelma said, the frown still in place, which made her appear even more bizarre. ''He has some kind of rash all over his back— big, nasty-looking welts.''

''Oh, my,'' Grace said, frowning also.

''I was hoping you had something I could put on them, some kind of antiseptic.''

''I'm sure I do,'' Grace said, glad for a reason to get away from Denton.

''Maybe you should call the doctor,'' Denton added, before she could so much as move a muscle.

Though he was talking to Zelma, Grace felt his smoldering gaze centered on her. She balled her fists, quelling the urge to throttle him. How dare he toy with her emotions as if she was his puppet on a string?

Cool it, she cautioned herself. Maybe she was making a mountain out of a molehill and she had misunderstood his motive. Maybe she should give him the benefit of the doubt and lighten up. Nah. She hadn't misunderstood. He'd been livid at the thought she'd messed up his chance to make a buck.

"Do you think it could be serious?" Zelma asked, a worried note in her voice.

Denton shrugged. "It might be caused by his medication."

"Well, he is on some new drugs since he had his attack."

"Let me go ahead and get you some ointment," Grace said, "then maybe you should call the doctor."

Zelma hesitated, then said to Grace, "Would you mind taking a look at it? I hate to ask, but under the circumstances—"

Grace patted her on the arm. "Say no more. I'll be glad to. I can't have anything happening to my favorite guests."

"You're going to have to stop spoiling that old coot."

Grace forced a smile. "Never."

"I'll let you look, too," Zelma said, facing Denton and bestowing a charming smile on him.

His lips twitched. "I'll pass. Two women making a fuss over poor old Ed is enough."

Zelma chuckled.

"Grace."

Because of Zelma, she didn't ignore him, though she refused to meet his eyes.

"We need to talk later, okay?"

"Maybe," she muttered before taking Zelma by the arm and pointing her down the hall toward her room.

Denton's expletive colored the air, but Grace kept right on moving.

"I think he's pissed," Zelma said, craning her neck and peering back over her shoulder.

Grace gritted her teeth. "He'll get over it."

Ass.

That word described him to a T, he thought, standing in his room and staring out the window after she'd turned her back on him and disappeared with Zelma, leaving him eating the dust of her vague comment.

She might not ever speak to him again, and he didn't blame her. Oh, she'd speak to him again, he assured himself, reality coming to his rescue. Under the circumstances, she didn't have much choice, but it wouldn't be the same.

He'd blown it.

And for no reason. The night they had shared had been incredible, a night he'd dreamed about often but never thought would happen. It had, then he'd rained on his own parade.

Before he had opened his eyes, he'd reached for her, only she hadn't been there. His eyes had popped open, thinking she might be in the bathroom. After checking, he realized she'd left.

Noticing the time, he figured she hadn't wanted to get caught sneaking out of his room after daylight for fear one of the guests might see her. But his disap-

pointment had been acute at being deprived of the
exquisite pleasure of rolling over and burying himself
back inside her warmth.

God, but she'd been so wet, so needy. Just like him.
Over and over. He'd lost count of the times they'd
made love, several of those times she'd been on top,
riding him until they had both cried out with release.
Sex had never been that satisfying.

Just thinking about Grace made him hard, made
him ache to dash down the hall, grab her and haul
her back to his room.

Sure, Hardesty, when pigs fly.

He'd had every intention of going to breakfast just
so he could be around her again, smell her, *touch her*.
Accidentally on purpose. But he'd gotten cold feet,
thinking that because she'd left his room without
awakening him she'd had regrets, that she was sorry
she'd given in to him.

With his mind playing those brutal tricks, he'd decided to go for a drive and think things through. If
anything, his thoughts had become more muddled
which was why, when he came to the nursery, he'd
stopped, especially since the carpenters were there
hammering away. Flora was outside, watching every
move they made.

He'd stopped and spoken to the men and to her.

"Oh, Denton, I can't believe this is really happening, that you've given this old woman a new lease on
life."

"My pleasure, Ms. Flora."

"Why did you do it?" She nudged him on the
shoulder. "Was it to impress Grace?"

He looked appalled. "Whatever gave you that
idea?"

"Huh! You can't fool an old broad like me who's been around the mountain a time or two. I haven't always been old and withered, sonny boy." She nudged him again and winked. "My old man and me played nasty many a time ourselves."

"Why, Flora Mantooth!"

"My point is I recognize that look when I see it."

He grinned, though his heart was beating much more rapidly than normal. "And what look would that be?"

"Like you could eat her with a spoon."

"I think your glasses need changing, Flora."

"You could do worse. That Grace is a favorite of just about everyone in Ruby."

"Shows Ruby has good taste."

"So make sure your intentions are honorable, sonny boy."

"I give you my word."

When he'd finally made it back to his vehicle, he'd felt as if he'd been gutted. He'd found it hard to believe that his feelings for Grace had shown to that extent. God, what had he gotten himself into?

That question had haunted him all the way back to the B&B and back to Grace. Suddenly he had ached to see her, to reassure himself that she wasn't sorry about what had happened between them.

It was shortly thereafter that he'd walked in and overheard her conversation with Ward. From that moment on, things had gone to hell in a handbasket.

Jealous. He was jealous of the client he hadn't even bothered to get back in touch with. Jealousy had been the driving force behind his knee jerk reaction to that call. He hadn't given a rip about the money, though he sure as hell wouldn't ever convince Grace of that, especially now. He'd just been so stunned that, first, it was the man he'd come to see whom she was talking to and, second, that he was asking her out.

The thought of anyone else touching her the way he'd touched her made him crazy. Jealousy aside, he had to face reality, too. If she and Ward were having an affair—that thought made his stomach revolt—then she just might feel the need to confess that she'd slept with him, Denton. In that case his deal would be nixed for sure. Somehow that didn't fit Grace's modus operandi, but then he really didn't know what made her tick.

So what if the deal went sour?

There were other deals with the same potential, even though this one might have been the one that bumped him up to partner. Partner, hell! If he didn't get his rear back to Dallas, he might not even have a job, much less a partnership.

But he wasn't ready to leave, not now for sure, not until he straightened this misunderstanding out with Grace. Then what? He broke out in sweat. Hell, he wouldn't think about that now. First things first.

Stewing wasn't getting the job done. He was going to have his say.

He found her on the front porch, a water bucket in hand, tending the plants. For a second he treated himself by just watching her. He took delight in everything about her from the lime-colored sleeveless dress that molded her slender figure to perfection, to her long, tapered legs that had plenty of room to move under the short hem and side slits, to her tousled hair that looked as if she'd just taken a tumble in the hay.

Which she had, earlier, with him.

Again he felt himself harden, wanting her, *needing* her.

Muttering a curse, Denton got out of his car and made his way up the steps. She finally turned and faced him, though she didn't say anything, her lovely features devoid of any expression. She wasn't going to make this easy for him, no sir.

Smothering a sigh, he crossed to the swing and sat down. "I'm sorry," he said simply.

"You should be."

"Does that mean you accept my apology?"

"No."

He swallowed another expletive. "I didn't mean it like it sounded. I don't care about the money."

"Yes, you do."

"Dammit, Grace!"

They both heard a door slam, their heads turning toward the sound simultaneously.

"Oh, dear," Grace whispered, clutching at her chest, her face going from red to stark white.

"Who's that?"

"The man you came to see, Ward Pearson."

Denton felt his own face drain of color. "Did you know he was coming?"

"No," she said in a barely audible tone.

"Hey, it's okay."

He watched as she took a deep, shuddering breath and plastered a smile on her face just as Ward's booted foot reached the first step.

"Howdy, folks," he said, tipping the edge of his Stetson, then glancing from one to the other as if he sensed the bad vibes in the air. "Am I intruding?" he asked in a low, gruff voice that sounded like cigarettes were his best friend.

Denton suspected that bourbon was the culprit instead.

"Hello, Ward," Grace responded, extending her hand, that plastic smile remaining in place.

He was long, tall drink of water, Denton thought, the consummate rancher, sporting a big truck and big bucks. He suspected that underneath his hat was a mop of gray hair or none at all. His face was severely tanned as if he lived in the sun. He wasn't a young man by any stretch. Still, he was nice-looking and was probably thought to be a great catch.

Pea-green jealousy almost kept Denton from rising and acknowledging Ward's presence with his own hand extended. "Denton Hardesty."

A shocked look narrowed Ward's eyes. "As in the investment broker?"

"One and the same," Denton said easily enough.

"How long have you been here?"

Denton picked up on the suspicion that now colored Ward's tone. Proceed with caution, Hardesty, not for your sake, but for Grace's. He would be the perfect man for her. When he was gone, Ward could step back in his rightful place. Again, that thought was so distasteful to Denton that he wanted to smash the other man's face.

Beautiful.

"Several days," Denton finally answered.

"I've left three messages for you, and they've gone unanswered." Ward's hostile gaze swung from Denton back to Grace.

Denton didn't have a comeback to that, so he said nothing.

"Now I can understand why," Ward declared flatly. "You've been otherwise occupied."

"Ward, please," Grace said, stepping forward.

Denton forced a curse back down his throat, then also moved forward. "Hey, it's not what you think."

Ignoring him, Ward whipped around and headed to his pickup.

Denton stood helplessly while Grace stared at Ward's back, a mortified look on her face.

Fourteen

"Grace—"

She held up her hand, cutting off his words. "Don't say anything, please."

"I know you're upset."

She glared at him. "That's an understatement."

"Look, I'm sorry if I screwed things up between you and Ward."

"Are you?"

He paused and stared at her for several long heartbeats. "No, dammit, I'm not."

"You're something else, Denton."

His mouth curled. "I deserved that, but while I know this seems to have gotten out of hand, it can all be straightened out."

"Don't worry about me." Her eyes flashed. "I can take care of myself. After all, I've been doing it for years."

"That's not the point."

Ignoring that, she said, "Why aren't you talking to Ward and trying to patch things up? Isn't that what this is all about?"

"No," he said, his jaw clenched so that his words sounded biting. "It's about you and me."

Grace shook her head in amazement. "You and me, huh? There is no you and me, Denton, and you know it." She paused. "Look, I'm going inside. I have things to do."

"Grace, don't do this. Let's talk about this."

She wanted to stay, to wallow in that pleading look, those huskily spoken words, but she knew he would just suck her under deeper, and she couldn't afford that. As it was she was barely hanging on to her sanity and her pride. One more push and she could topple over that edge.

"I need some space, Denton. Maybe we'll talk later." She paused again, her gaze raking over his. "Meanwhile, I suggest you call Ward and straighten things out. After all, that's why you're still here."

Before he could reply, she turned and went inside, not releasing her pent-up breath until she reached her room and closed the door.

She had just gotten out of the tub, where she had soaked in bubbles up to her neck, and dressed in a pair of shorts and loose blouse when the phone rang. For a second she was tempted to ignore it, but again, running a business that depended heavily on the phone, she couldn't afford that luxury.

"Hello," she said, trying to force some brightness into her tone.

"Grace, it's Ward."

Great.

Sinking onto the chaise lounge, she clutched the receiver tightly. "I'm glad you called."

"You are?" His tone held genuine surprise.

"Of course. We're friends."

"Look, I acted like a horse's behind, and I want to apologize for that."

"Hey, you don't owe me an apology. If anything, I owe you one."

"The hell you do. I acted like a jealous you-know-what, and I had no right."

True, she wanted to say, but she didn't. Ward was such a nice guy, but he wasn't the one for her, Denton or no Denton. She had to make him understand that without hurting or humiliating him further.

"But when I saw you and Hardesty," he added, regaining her attention. "I lost my cool."

"Denton's an old friend," Grace said lamely.

"Judging from the way he was looking at you, he'd like to be more."

How she wished that were so, but she knew better. Denton wanted to make love to her, not make a future. On the other hand, Ward wanted both. Too bad she loved the wrong man. Tears suddenly gathered in her eyes though she fought them back.

She wasn't about to cry over Denton. She'd wasted enough tears on him already to last a lifetime.

"He's just passing through, Ward. He'll be leaving as soon as the two of you meet."

"I don't know so much about that."

She felt herself panic. No way was she going to be responsible for Denton not getting his deal or at least having a shot at it. While he stressed he didn't care, she did. "Oh, please, I'd feel awful if you two didn't get together because of me."

"Hardesty might see that differently."

"Please, Ward, leave me out of this, okay?"

"Okay, honey, whatever you say." He paused. "Are you ever going to change your mind about me, Grace?"

She heard the pain in his voice and hated that she was the cause of it. But she couldn't lie to him. She couldn't make herself love him no matter how hard she wanted to. Her heart belonged elsewhere and always had.

"No, Ward," she said as sweetly as possible. "You're a great guy and I value our friendship—"

"I get it. You don't have to draw me a picture."

She flushed. "I'm sorry."

"You don't have to be that, either. I just figured it was time I knew exactly where I stood."

"There's someone out there for you," Grace said. "I just know there is."

"Yeah, Ruby's full of single women."

Through the pain she heard the humor, which she returned by chuckling herself. "Just like it's full of single men."

"Well, if friendship is all there is, then I'll take it."

"Thanks, Ward," she responded, a catch in her voice.

"Now, moving on, we need to meet about this nuclear plant crap. I've had my ear to the ground, and the rumbling's growing louder that Ruby's pretty high on the list."

"I'm ready to meet and load our guns. Just let me know the time and place."

"I'll talk to you later, then."

She was already drained, but now she felt really

zapped of energy. What a day. First her encounter with Denton, then Ward, then Denton and Ward together. No one deserved that. Suddenly she felt the urge to scream. When had her peaceful life disappeared?

When Denton drove into town.

Sighing, Grace got up and walked to the French doors that led onto the balcony outside her room. She opened them, stepped out into the refreshing spring air and clung to the railing. The evening was lovely, she told herself, made for lovers.

Stop it. She couldn't afford to let that thought run rampant or she'd be in a world of hurt. But it was hard when all she could think about was how it felt to have Denton inside her again, how she longed to experience that hard heat every day for the rest of her life.

Not going to happen.

Breathing deeply, the scent of the flowers heightened her senses, making her edgier than ever. Maybe a cup of hot tea on the front porch would soothe her soul. She would love to visit with Zelma and Ed; they never failed to buoy up her spirits. But they had finally gotten off to Austin and wouldn't be back until late.

As for Denton, she figured he was in his room, walking the floor with his ear glued to the phone, tending to business.

What she wanted to know was when he was leaving.

Surely he couldn't afford to remain in Ruby much longer. His boss was bound to start hollering for real and demand that he return to the office. There was just so much one could accomplish by phone.

Hopefully, now that Ward had returned and they had met, Denton would make the deal of all deals, she told herself with sarcasm, then fire up his BMW and head back to Dallas, back to civilization, as he called it.

Taking another whiff of the flowers, Grace made her way back inside, but she didn't linger. She headed downstairs to the kitchen where she made some flavored tea, then went onto the front porch only to pull up short.

Denton occupied the swing.

If she hadn't had a firm grip on the cup, she would've dropped it.

"Oh," she murmured, suddenly conscious of the fact that she didn't have on a bit of makeup and her hair was mussed. More important, she didn't have on a bra. Under any other circumstances it wouldn't have bothered her, except her nipples had gone instantly erect at the sight of him.

Feeling her mouth go dry, she swallowed hard. Even after he was gone, every time she walked out the front door, she would still see him in that swing looking like the big, sexy hunk he was.

Damn him and his intrusion in her life.

"You're not happy to see me." His words were a flat statement of fact.

"No, I'm not," she said with equal bluntness.

His features suddenly looked tired and strained. "I couldn't stay cooped up in my room a second longer."

"That's how I felt," she admitted reluctantly, not wanting to dwell on his long, bare legs splayed out in front of him.

"You can sit down, you know."

"I know." She didn't move an inch.

"Even on the swing with me."

Was that humor lurking in his tone, or had she imagined it? It didn't matter; either way she was not in the mood to indulge him.

"I know that, too," she muttered, fighting the urge to dash back in the house like a frightened doe. Instead, she stiffened her spine and forced her demeanor to remain unruffled. He was not about to get the upper hand here. This was her porch. If anyone was the invader, it was him.

Besides, she couldn't run from him and the emotions he evoked in her, not when she'd let him make love to her. To play the outraged virgin at this point was a bit ludicrous.

"Are you in love with him?"

At first his words didn't register. Then it hit her what he'd said, and she stared at him wide-eyed. "What?" she asked simply because she was so stunned.

He released a harsh sigh. "Don't make me repeat it. Next time, I might choke on the words."

"Are you referring to Ward?"

"Of course." He leaned his head to one side while his eyes stabbed her. "Who else?"

Loaded question, one that she would dodge at all costs.

"You know I'm not in love with him," she retorted, red-faced.

"How the hell would I know that?"

"If I had been, I wouldn't have made love to you."

"God, Grace," he said, standing, his voice tormented, "I never meant to invade your space like this."

"Is that your way of telling me you're sorry we made love?" The words came out a raspy whisper.

"No," he said in a strangled tone. "I—"

"I know what you're thinking, that I'm a love-starved old maid who's grateful for the crumbs you threw me."

He closed the distance between them in one long stride and clutched her arm. "That's hogwash!"

She peered down at his hand on her flesh then back up at him. Green eyes lingered on her brown ones, both dark and filled with secrets. "Is it?" Her voice was broken.

"Yes," he whispered.

Fifteen

His lips were everywhere.

And she didn't want the sweet torment to end, even though she craved to feel the hard strength of him inside her.

She had no idea how they had gotten from the porch to his room, to his big bed. Yes, she did, she told herself, only she hated to admit the weakness that had made her give in to the burning need he created inside her.

When he'd grasped her arm, stared down at her and seduced her with those hot, green eyes, she had turned to putty. She remembered parting her lips then hearing him groan before his lips ground into hers—hard and deep.

The next thing she knew they were on the bed, naked, laving each other with mouths and tongues.

"Oh, Grace, I want you so much," he rasped, closing her mind to everything except him and what he was doing to her body.

"Oh, yes," she whispered, squirming under the feel of his tongue between each toe before moving up the inside of her leg to the apex of her thighs.

He had already made her crazy, having kneaded and suckled her breasts until they were full and wet with the juices from his lips.

Now she gasped and grabbed a handful of dark hair as his tongue made contact with her wet center. "Ohh," she gasped again when blessed relief instantly flooded through her.

"I love pleasing you this way." The rasp of his voice sounded as if he'd just swallowed sandpaper as he shifted his position so that his full-blown manhood replaced his tongue.

"Denton, Denton," she muttered incoherently.

"I can't wait any longer." His hungry eyes were on her.

"Neither can I," she cried, touching the tip of him, guiding him inside her.

Holding her with strength and intensity, flesh met flesh and hips rocked against hips until both their cries of satisfaction rent the air.

What a perfect spring day to be at the nursery, perusing the plants, Grace thought, that is, if one liked tiptoeing among carpenters. She almost smiled.

She'd had to escape the house. The walls felt as if they were closing in on her. She didn't want to think about Denton. Yet he was all she did think about. Consequently, her nerves had been driving her, rather than the other way around. That was when she'd found Zelma sitting on the front porch, swinging while Ed slept. Off the top of her head, she'd asked Zelma if she'd like to go to the nursery with her.

Zelma hadn't hesitated. Now they had just arrived, and Grace was still reeling from shock. The old dilapidated premises had received a face-lift, though the transformation was not totally complete. Denton had certainly lived up to his promise to Flora, which both relieved and pleased Grace.

She'd been afraid...

"Honey child, you ought to snag that man."

"That's what I've been trying to tell her," Zelma said, inclining her head and giving Grace a knowing look. "For more reasons than one." She paused and swept her hands in a circle. "Why, just look at what all he's doing for Flora here."

"Don't that beat all," Flora added, a dazed sound to her voice. "If I was just a tad younger, he could sure eat crackers in my bed."

Zelma grinned, then winked at Grace.

Grace quelled a sigh, staving off the urge to throttle her friend, actually both of them, she corrected. They were ganging up on her, and it wasn't fair.

"So?" Flora's tone was as pointed as her eyes.

"So, nothing," Grace replied, with as much indifference as she could muster while at the same time masking her irritation. The last thing she wanted was to hurt the old women's feelings. Still, Denton was an off-limits subject, considering the volatile nature of their relationship.

If they only knew she'd spent the night with Denton hot and hard inside her....

"Are you all right, dear?" Zelma demanded into the sudden silence, her gaze concentrated on Grace.

"You look sort of peaked, like Ed does sometimes when he can't catch his breath."

"I'm...fine," Grace said lamely. "Just felt dizzy for a sec."

"It's all that talk about gettin' herself a man," Flora said without pulling any punches. "Why, that rancher's been trying to rope her for months now, and she won't have nothin' to do with him. And he's got more money than God."

"Flora!" Grace shot her a look. "Give it a rest."

"Well, I don't know anything about this rancher," Zelma chimed in, "but I think you've lost your mind not to go after Denton."

"And just what, pray tell, would I do with him?" Grace asked before she thought.

"Marry him," Flora said bluntly.

Grace made a strangled sound. "Yeah, right."

"Well, that's not so far-fetched, my dear," Zelma put in. "The looks he often gives you are hot enough to scorch the earth. So don't play the innocent with me."

Flora bobbed her head up and down like a cork. "Or me. I've seen the same thing."

"Hey, you two." Grace held up her hands. "Cut me some slack, okay? Denton is simply passing through."

"We'll see," Zelma said loftily.

Again Grace wanted to throttle both women as they turned and winked at each other as if she didn't see them, as if she didn't know what was going on. But it really didn't matter. So what if she indulged them in their little game of romance? They were playing cupid and having a ball doing it. Why spoil their fun time? She knew the truth, and that was all that counted.

Despite the fact that Denton might look at her with undeniable heat, that hot streak would burn itself out just as soon as he climbed in his BMW and headed for Dallas. Suddenly a tight squeeze on her heart robbed her of her next breath.

But she recovered, not wanting to call more attention to herself by having an anxiety attack.

Grace peered at her watch, then back up to Zelma. "I'd best get what I came after and go back to the house. I have work to do."

"Speaking of working," Flora said, "I hope it won't take these fellows much longer to wrap things up around here."

Grace smiled. "I'm sure it won't, at least not the way they're working."

"I still can't believe this is happening," Flora said, her cataract-clouded eyes wide with wonder. "It makes me kind of scared at the thought of operating such a fancy place now."

Grace hugged her. "You'll be just fine. However, you will have to hire someone to help you, I would imagine. Your business is going to double or better."

"Oh, Lordy," Flora wheezed, grabbing her chest. "I hope I'm up to the challenge."

Zelma gave her a pointed but reassuring look. "Sure you are."

"Come on, dear," Grace said, a lilt in her voice, "strut your stuff. Pick me out some new plants for my porch."

A short time later Grace was back at the B&B, digging in one of the pots on the side porch. Zelma and Ed had decided to go back into Austin, and Ralph was in his usual spot in front of his computer. The only one out of place was Denton.

She had no idea where he was, except that maybe he'd gone to try to smooth things over with Ward, still hoping to get his business. When she'd driven up from the nursery and his car had been gone, her heart had dropped to her knees, thinking that perhaps he'd already cut out to Dallas without so much as a good-bye.

In her heart of hearts she had known that wasn't true. There would be real closure this time, but it still wouldn't lessen the emptiness, the pain of losing him again. But when she had involved herself with him, she had known the end result. Nothing had changed, despite another night of passion in his arms.

As before, she had left his bed and crept into hers. However, this time she hadn't escaped without him knowing. He had grabbed her arm, which had frozen her to the side of the bed. Without peering back at him, she'd whispered, "What?"

"We have to talk," he'd responded.

"Not now," she said, a break in her voice.

"When?""

"I'm...not sure."

"Later today?" His tone was low but forceful.

She licked her bottom lip. "We'll see."

"Grace—" This time there was exasperation in his tone.

"I don't see that we have anything to talk about."

He withdrew his hand and muffled an expletive.

That was when she walked out. Now, as she dug in the dirt, she longed for the feeling of well-being that always stole over her. It didn't come. She remained uptight, wired and close to tears.

Battling back the threat of tears, Grace jabbed her trowel deeper in the dirt.

"My, but that must be some difficult soil."

Startled by the unexpected sound of a voice, Grace jerked her head up and stared into the face of a man she'd never seen before. He had more than his share of unkempt hair, which she suspected was prematurely gray as he seemed rather young. He was of medium height, but nothing else was medium about him, certainly not his girth. It was distended far too much to be comfortable.

Though she sensed his impatience, his grin was friendly enough.

"Are you here to inquire about lodging?" she asked, straightening to full height.

"No wonder he's not back," the man mumbled.

Grace pushed a loose stand of hair back and blinked. "Excuse me?"

"I'm Todd Joseph," he said suddenly, extending his hand. "Denton's boss. Is he around?"

Grace felt her stomach hollow as she removed her gloves and forced a smile.

"Mr. Pearson's out on the range, working cattle."

Denton smothered a sigh. "I guess it'll be late when he gets back."

"If he does at all." The housekeeper shrugged. "Sometimes he spends the night out there."

"Well, tell him Denton Hardesty came by and that I'll catch him later."

The lady nodded, then closed the door.

When he returned to his vehicle, Denton didn't crank it. He merely sat there, feeling limp and de-

flated, something that made him want to kick butt—
his in particular.

He rubbed his head, feeling it pop, as though he
had a zinger of a hangover. He had to get his act
together. He couldn't continue to indulge himself to
this degree or he might as well chuck his job.

For what? He sneered. Dance attendance to Grace?
Yes, dammit.

Why not? Since he'd been in Ruby with nothing
but great weather, great food, great company, he'd
become a new person. He'd become humanized. Seeing that smile on Flora's face and feeling her wet kiss
on his cheek had done something good for his soul,
something that hadn't happened to him in a long time,
far too long to even remember the feeling.

Damn sad.

So what did this mellow feeling mean? Was he
trying to convince himself that he wanted a steady
diet of Ruby and its laid-back lifestyle? No. He didn't
think so. What he did want, however, was a steady
diet of Grace.

He'd rather be with her than anyplace on earth.
What he felt for Grace was more than the constant
gnawing of sex. He was smitten with her every move,
her infectious laughter, her flashing eyes, her sharp
tongue.

All wrapped up together, she presented an enchant-
ing package. And he didn't want to leave Ruby without it. *Without her.*

Only after he felt the throbbing in his head ease
some, did he start the powerful engine. But instead of
heading toward the B&B, he went by the nursery. He
had no intention of stopping. Once Flora got her
claws into him, all avenues of escape were usually

blocked. He grinned without restraint. Most times he didn't even mind that, even enjoyed jawing with the sharp-witted old woman.

Not today. He merely wanted to keep an eye on the workers, to make sure they were there and working. Since he'd struck out with Pearson, something he hadn't been looking forward to, anyway, he couldn't wait to get back to Grace, test her temperature following last night's lovemaking session—more incredible than the last time.

How could he leave her?

Sweat, followed by cold chills, broke through his skin. He had no choice. No matter how much he liked it here, he couldn't stay. Not indefinitely, that is. Not even much longer, either, he reminded himself. Already he was pushing the envelope with Todd, who blew smoke out of his ears every time they talked, which was becoming several times a day.

In reality he knew he couldn't continue to operate his million-dollar-plus business from afar. Yet he hated like hell to leave without Grace.

Suddenly he braked and pulled off the road. Why the hell hadn't he thought of that before? Of course. That was the answer. That would work. All he needed was the quality time to pull it off.

He turned onto Live Oak Lane only to groan, then let go of another expletive. None other than his boss's green Cadillac was parked in the drive. Todd himself was parked on the front porch, seemingly deep in conversation with Grace.

"Damn!"

A face-to-face confrontation with his boss had been something he'd hoped to avoid. Didn't appear things were going to work that way. Todd waited for him to get out and make his way onto the porch. Denton figured his boss was angry. The line around his mouth and his stiff stance said as much.

"I was hoping it wouldn't come to this," Todd said without preamble, glaring at him.

Ignoring him, Denton faced Grace and smiled. "Would you excuse us?"

Without returning his look, she said, "No problem."

Once they were alone, both men were silent. Todd was the first to speak, his tone sardonic, "I'm assuming that piece of work is why you're still here."

Denton stood his ground, not so much as flinching. "You got that right."

Sixteen

"**W**ell, I'll have to hand it you, she's a looker."

For some reason that observation irritated Denton no end. But then, having his boss show up here in Ruby was irritant enough without bringing Grace into the equation.

"However, I don't think she's worth throwing your career down the toilet." Without being asked, Todd then lowered his heavy frame into the swing, propping a foot over his knee. "I haven't seen any woman worth that." His tone was filled with acid.

"And you think that's the case here?" Denton asked, holding on to his temper by a mere thread.

Todd sneered. "I think you know the answer to that."

"What the hell are you doing here?" Denton demanded, noticing that Todd appeared far too comfortable in that swing. Hopefully, Grace wouldn't pull one of her hospitality stunts and bring out a tray loaded with her special goodies and her flavored iced tea. Todd wouldn't budge another inch for sure.

On second thought, he'd be surprised if Grace reappeared. She had sensed the climate when she'd walked off and wouldn't want to get involved in a discussion between him and his boss.

"I'm here to help you come to your senses," Todd said flatly.

"I wasn't aware that I'd lost them."

Todd snorted, and this time his belly shook. "Only a woman would come between you and money."

Denton felt his stomach burn. "You don't know what you're talking about."

"Are you in love with her?"

"Dammit, Todd, mind your own business."

"Hey, that's exactly what I'm doing, good buddy. In case you haven't noticed, we're pretty closely joined at the hip, which means your business is my business."

"So the partnership's still in the offing?" After he asked that, Denton held his breath for fear of what the answer would be. He wouldn't blame Todd if he did can him. He definitely hadn't been his usual, driven, professional self since returning to Ruby. But he didn't need Todd to tell him that.

"Only if you get your rear back to Dallas and on your accounts."

Denton felt a flush steal into his cheeks, more from anger than embarrassment. He could hold his own against this man regardless of who he was or what he represented. When he'd gone to work for Todd, he'd been looking for a job. He could do so again. Still...

"So are you in love?" Todd pressed.

"No."

"Well, you gotta be in lust then. Nothing else would keep you in this godforsaken place."

"This is where I grew up." Denton's tone was on the defensive, and he didn't know why. He'd knocked Ruby more times than he cared to admit. But then that was before he'd returned and Grace— Nipping that thought in the bud, he let go of a pent-up sigh.

Todd's voice hardened. "I wouldn't be bragging about that."

"Okay, you've made your point," Denton muttered. "You've driven here and slapped my wrist."

"I came here because I want to know what the hell's going on," Todd stressed. "You know how much I depend on you, and it's been awful without you in the office. Any moment now several deals are threatening to go to hell in a handbasket."

"I still haven't made personal contact with Ward Pearson," Denton said, hoping to take some of the heat off himself and calm Todd down.

"And why not?"

"He had to leave town and has just returned." That wasn't all a lie, Denton reminded himself, though he couldn't quite look his friend straight in the eye. "In fact, I just tried to visit with him, and he's riding his range."

"Gawd."

"You're in the hill country, remember?"

"I feel like I'm on another bloody planet."

Denton almost smiled.

"So see Pearson tomorrow, wrap up that deal and head for North Texas."

Todd's words weren't phrased as a question but rather a statement of fact. And even though there was no overt threat, Denton heard one in the undertones. With Todd, push had definitely come to shove.

"If he's back, I'll see what I can do." Denton's tone was calm but firm. While he agreed with Todd about his absence, he wasn't about to let him think he could browbeat him into submission. That old dog wouldn't hunt. Anyway, before he left Ruby, he had something to take care of, but Todd didn't have to know that.

"If you snag the deal, our company will be flying high."

"And I'll be full partner," Denton added to the sentence.

"That was the deal." Todd fell silent, then peered up at him. "You still haven't told me what's going on between you and that honey inside."

"And I'm not going to, either."

"Ah, so you do have the hots for her." Todd grinned, then stood. "Can't say I blame you."

"Get out of here."

"Aren't you going to offer me some refreshments?" Todd asked in a taunting voice.

He nodded his head across the street. "The station sells drinks."

"Man, you do have it bad."

"Don't push your luck, my friend," Denton said in a gruff tone.

"No problem. I'm going. Give your little lady my best regards." Todd slapped Denton on the shoulder. "Just remember what you went through with your ex."

"Stuff it, Todd," Denton muttered harshly.

"Oh, speaking of exes. Yours called."

"Marsha?"

"Yep."

"What the hell did she want?"

"More money, she said."

Denton laughed with biting humor. "She's crazy!"

"I agree. She took you to the cleaners when you divorced."

"Wrong. I chose to give her the cleaners," Denton declared. "There's a difference."

Todd shrugged his massive shoulders. "Whatever."

"What did you tell her?"

"That you'd call her."

Denton scowled. "One day I'll do you a favor."

Todd threw back his head and laughed, then ambled down the steps. "I'll see you in Big D."

Grace would have loved to be a fly on the wall out on the porch, she thought, as she mixed the dough for rolls. On second thought, maybe not. She could imagine the barbs zinging between the two men. Her delicate ears probably couldn't have survived. She smiled at such an absurd thought. Still, she figured the climate was as cold as the Arctic. She had sensed that immediately.

Even though Todd What's-His-Name seemed like an amicable enough guy, he was as hard-nosed and driven as Denton, or he wouldn't have shot off in search of his prodigal employee.

Grace's smile suddenly fled as did the warmth around her heart that had remained with her following their intense but sweet night of lovemaking. She knew he didn't love her. Yet she'd never felt so loved or cherished in her life.

And he would be leaving. Today, most likely. Maybe with Todd.

This time her heart almost stopped completely, and for an instant the room spun, but, taking several deep breaths, Grace regrouped and everything righted, except her heart.

She tackled the dough like it was her enemy, kneading it until it was in stringy pieces. Then realizing what she was doing, she stopped, washed her hands then patted her face with cold wet fingers. She had returned to the kitchen with every intention of preparing a tray and taking it to the porch, only to change her mind. She hadn't wanted to overstep her bounds. Too, Denton certainly hadn't been in the entertaining mode.

Once the dough was back intact and the rolls in the oven, Grace stood still for the longest time. And listened. Finally she heard an engine crank. Swaying, she held on to the countertop and waited.

When Denton drove off, part of her would leave with him. But he couldn't stay, the rational part of her mind cried back. That wouldn't work, either. He would soon be miserable and make her miserable, as well.

So Todd's arrival was a godsend. Denton had to go before he set up permanent residence in her soul.

"My, something sure smells good in here."

Grace forced a smile on Ed and Zelma. "You say that every morning."

Ed chuckled. "That's 'cause it's true every morning." He paused and turned to Zelma. "We're sure going to miss this, dear."

Zelma poked him in the ribs. "You just don't know when to keep your mouth shut, you old coot."

Grace sobered, her eyes shifting from one to the other. "You're leaving." Her words came out sounding like a death knell.

"Oh, honey," Zelma said in a conciliatory tone, rushing over and giving Grace a hug. "You knew this time had to come. We're coming back, though."

"When?"

"Moving, in fact."

Grace's eyes lighted. "Oh, Zelma, that's wonderful."

Zelma winked at Ed, who was heading for the bowl of fruit on the counter and helping himself. "We told the kids last night."

"And?" Grace held her breath.

Grace hesitated, then grinned. "They said go for it."

"All right!"

Grace knew Denton had walked into the room, though he hadn't said a word. His animal magnetism never failed to precede him. "What's so exciting in here?"

Zelma turned and, after hugging him, told him the news.

His gaze rested briefly but deeply on Grace, who somehow kept herself from flushing. "I know you're thrilled."

"Beyond words," she said softly.

Their eyes lingered a second longer before she turned away, troubled by the shadows that lurked in his. She wondered when he would tell her he was leaving, as well.

Zelma actually voiced the question. "So, when are you heading back to the city?"

"Soon."

"Didn't you just have a visitor?" Zelma asked, apparently not ready to let him off the hook so easily.

If her insides hadn't been in such turmoil and there hadn't been so much at stake, Grace would've smiled at seeing Denton on the hot seat.

"Zelma," Ed said, "that's none of your business."

"Oh, poppycock. Nothing's a secret around here."

"Guess not," Denton said drolly.

"So, why didn't you invite your friend to breakfast?"

"Zelma!"

She flapped her hand at him. "Oh, Ed, give it a rest."

Grace's eyes met Denton's again. This time there was a smile in them, and he winked, melting her heart on the spot.

"Despite my better half," Zelma said to Denton, "I'm not letting you off the hook."

"That was my boss from Dallas, who's after my hide to leave here."

"Hey, everyone," Grace said suddenly, unable to bear the turn in conversation, for fear she'd fall apart in front of everyone. "Let's eat. I've set us up on the porch."

For the next hour, conversation was impersonal and lively. Even Ralph joined them and added a couple of author anecdotes that were humorous. Just as everyone was finishing, Connie arrived.

Denton, along with everyone else, excused himself and went to his quarters. A short time later Grace heard him on the phone. She forced herself to concentrate on her business, but it was hard, especially when she knew her world was about to come crashing down on her again.

She was losing all her guests at one time, which happened often. Zelma and Ed were packing and loading up. And while she was saddened by their departure, the fact that they were coming back to live in Ruby eased the pain. Ralph was also leaving, having completed his novel right on deadline.

As far as Denton was concerned, she expected him to fly out of his room at any time, briefcase in hand and climb into his BMW.

"We'll see you soon," Zelma said one last time and after one final hug, before getting into the car. "Meanwhile, we'll keep in touch by phone." She pulled Grace's head closer and whispered, "Don't you dare let that hunk just waltz out of your life. I know there's something going on between you two, and I don't mean just between the sheets, either."

With her face scalding-red, Grace stepped back. "One of these days…"

Zelma merely chuckled as Ed backed out of the drive.

The remainder of the day passed like molasses running uphill, despite the fact she was so busy with bookwork and housework. Yet she kept listening for Denton to make his move. He didn't. If he left his room, she was unaware of it, though she did leave and run some errands.

Now, as she was about to make her way upstairs to take her bath, Denton's door opened. She paused mid-stride, their gazes meeting and holding. He looked exhausted and rumpled. She'd never seen him quite so disheveled.

"I know, don't say it." He shoved his hand through his hair, further mussing it. "I look like the bloody wrath."

"Okay, you do, but I won't say it."

A smile flirted on his lips. "Are you alone?"

"Yes." The fact that she was now alone in the house with Denton was something she refused to think about.

"Would you like to go out to dinner?"

Her eyes widened. "I thought—" She clamped her lips together.

"Are you ready for me to leave?" His eyes were broodingly intense.

She swallowed. "No. Of course not."

"So what about dinner?"

"Why don't I fix something here instead?"

His eyes raked slowly over her. "You wouldn't mind?"

"Uh, no, not in the least." Her voice sounded breathless, but she couldn't help it. "I'd rather."

"I'll clean up, then, and join you."

Their gazes lingered on each other for another moment, then he turned and went back into his room. She wilted against the doorjamb, her mind splintering in a million different directions.

What was that all about?

Seventeen

Despite the hovering tension, the meal went off without a hitch. As he had at breakfast, he made her laugh with several stories about clients. She in turn related some of the weirdos she'd had at the B&B. All in all, the intimate dinner went much better than she'd expected, though by the time she poured their coffee, she thought her insides would explode.

He'd been so close, so within touching distance, yet she couldn't touch him. Once she did, she wouldn't stop. She sensed he felt the same, as he seemed to make it a point not to make direct contact with her skin, only her eyes, devouring her through them.

They had just settled down in the living room with coffee when the doorbell chimed.

Denton frowned. "Who the hell...?"

"I have no earthly idea," Grace said, getting up.

"Don't answer it," Denton muttered to her back.

Ignoring him, she opened the door. Roger Gooseby, the mayor and grocer, stood on the porch, hat in hand.

"May I come in?" he asked without preamble.

"Of course," Grace told him, fighting off a sinking feeling in the pit of her stomach. She didn't want anyone or anything to encroach on her last few hours with Denton. Time with him was at a premium.

Once Roger's tall, lean frame had cleared the entrance, she gestured for him to be seated, but not before introducing him to Denton.

"Would you like me to leave?" Denton asked.

"No," Grace said quickly. "It's about the nuclear plant, isn't it, Roger?"

"That it is," he said, barely able to mask his fury.

"What's happened?"

"The powers-that-be are apparently looking at us real close, like second from the top."

"Oh, dear," Grace said, glancing at Denton then back to Roger.

"When I get back to Dallas, I may be able to help," Denton put in.

"You think you can help?" Roger's tone was brusque.

Denton stretched his legs in front of him. "Maybe. I have a connection that might make a difference."

Roger's leathered face brightened. "We'd sure appreciate anything you could do. Meanwhile, Grace, I've talked to several others, and we'd like you to be our spokesperson, travel to Washington, if need be."

"That's a smart move, Mr. Gooseby," Denton said.

"Roger," the grocer corrected. "Formalities don't play around here."

"No."

At first Grace knew neither man had heard her answer. They were too busy becoming chummy, which was a waste of time. Once he left Ruby, Denton wouldn't ever see Roger again.

"What did you say?" the mayor asked, cutting his head around.

"No." There. She said it again.

"But...but why not?" Roger spluttered.

Denton's gaze pinned her. "Yeah, why not? You'd be the perfect one, considering your personality and your devotion to this town."

Grace shook her head vigorously. "I'll do anything else, but I won't be in charge."

"We sure need you, Grace," Roger said, his tone gruff. "If this thing doesn't get nipped in the bud, Ruby's going to be in a world of hurt."

"I know, Roger." Grace paused a second and rubbed her temple. "I'm in business, too. But I'm not the right person."

"I disagree," he countered bluntly. "I think you're the perfect person."

"I'm sorry, but I won't do it."

He scratched his head, then released a harsh sigh. "Well, I guess that's that. If you change your mind, holler. Meanwhile, we'll try and come up with an alternate person and plan."

He stood then, and Grace followed suit, extending her hand and giving him a forced smile. "It will work out. It just has to for all our sakes."

"Let's pray." Roger nodded in Denton's direction, then added, "I'll see myself out."

Once the mayor was gone, the room fell silent. Grace couldn't bring herself to look at Denton, knowing he was disappointed in her. His disappointment seemed to roll off him in waves. The fact that she cared what he thought made her furious.

"If you aren't willing to fight for Ruby, then why don't you leave?"

"And go where?" she bit back sarcastically.

"To Dallas?"

She gasped. "To Dallas?"

"It's not another planet, you know," he pointed out on a dry note.

"As far as I'm concerned it is." She paused, then added, "And just why would I even consider such a thing?"

"Because I ask you to."

Grace went weak all over. "And what would I do?"

He didn't hesitate. "Live with me."

For a moment she had thought— "As your mistress?" Voicing those words made her sick to her stomach. Why couldn't he say he loved her? Because he doesn't. He never has and never will. How much longer was she going to let this man have charge over her body and soul?

"That's not the term I'd prefer to use."

Grace laughed a hollow laugh. "Oh, really. In any case, I don't think so."

He flushed. "Dammit, Grace—"

"I'm not leaving Ruby. Ever."

"Why the hell not?" he exploded. "You're wasting your time and your life in this godforsaken place."

"How would you know?" she lashed back. "You still don't know anything about me."

"I know enough to know you don't belong here."

"Instead I belong there as your little bimbette."

He cursed. "It wouldn't be that way, and you know it."

"I don't intend to ever be your mistress or any man's. Is there anything about *that* you don't understand?"

"Dammit!"

He might as well not have spoken. She was on a roll and didn't intend to stop until she'd had her say. "Man, oh, man, it sure didn't take you long to start bad-mouthing the peace and quiet."

"We're not talking about me," Denton countered, his lips white around the outer edge.

He was not happy, Grace knew, but neither was she. "Well, again, I love what I do and where I'm doing it."

He scoffed. "You'd love it in the city."

Livid, she retorted, "This may come as a shock to you, but I haven't always lived here in this godforsaken town as you call it." She paused and watched his nostrils flare, knowing she'd pushed the right button. "I was an assistant district attorney in Houston until I couldn't stand the rat race any longer and walked away."

Her words fell into the room with the punch of a huge anchor falling overboard on a ship. Denton merely stared at her in disbelief, his jaw slack. "You're putting me on."

"You know better than that," she snapped.

He rubbed his slightly grizzled chin in an agitated move. "You're an attorney?"

Again there was shock, which he didn't bother to conceal, adding to her fury. "Is that so hard to believe?"

"Yes," he said bluntly, "considering your lifestyle now."

"Well, it's a fact."

"What made you give all that up?"

"When I started having anxiety attacks," she said with simple honesty.

He blew out a breath. "That's certainly a kicker. But couldn't you have just cut back—"

"I made my choice, Denton," she responded softly, "and I've never regretted it."

"You mount a mean defense, Grace Simmons."

This time a smile flirted with her lips. "After all, that's what attorneys do."

He stared at her long and hard with an unreadable expression in his eyes. "I still say you're wasted here."

"And I still say that's *not* going to change."

They glared at each other suddenly, their breathing elevated.

"You know you want me."

His thickly spoken words almost buckled her knees. "I never denied that," she whispered, toying with her lower lip.

He groaned, his eyes darkening. "All I can think of right now is how nice it would be to have you in my bed every night and every morning."

"Why are you doing this?" Her tone was agonized.

"Because I can't stand the thought of being without you, of leaving you." He closed the distance between them, reached for her hand and placed it on his crotch. Though she sucked in her breath, she didn't move her hand. She reveled in the feeling of ecstasy his pulsating hardness was bringing her.

"Then don't," she finally managed to get out, lifting her eyes and meeting his, all the while keeping her hand on him.

"Don't what?" He sounded as if the words were dug out of him.

"Don't leave."

"I have to."

"No, you don't." Her hand squeezed him.

He groaned again and closed his eyes for a brief second. When he opened them again, they were dark with passion. "My job's in Dallas."

"Mine is here."

"You're making me crazy."

"Not any crazier than you're making me."

"I'll be good to you, I promise," he pressed urgently. "You won't ever want for a thing."

Except your love.

As though she'd been burned, she dropped her hand and stepped back. His eyes narrowed as he sucked in his breath and held it. "I don't want for a thing now, Denton. And I'm my own person, not a kept woman."

He let an expletive fly. "Don't you think that's a bit outdated?"

"Maybe."

"Hell, people move in together every day. It's no big deal."

"It is to me," she countered quietly.

"Grace—"

She held up her hand and cut him off. "Enough. I'm going to bed."

A heavy silence followed her words.

"I'm not giving up."

"You're wasting your time. But I'll see you in the morning—if you're still here, that is."

Another stinging expletive followed her out the door.

"You won't regret this, Ward."

"I'd better not."

Denton withdrew his hand. "I'll fax you all the necessary papers when they're done."

"Whatever. Just as long as I don't have to go to that hellhole for anything."

Denton shook his head, wondering if everyone in Ruby felt that way about cities. "I'm sure it's all doable by machines."

Ward shoved his hat back on his head and squinted his eyes. They had just left the rancher's big, airy kitchen where they'd cussed and discussed the deal until Denton had finally gotten his name on the dotted line. Now they were outside, standing beside Denton's BMW.

"One more thing," Ward said, his crusty voice sounding even crustier.

"Anything."

"You'd better handle her with gentle, loving care."

Denton blinked. "Excuse me?"

"You know who and what I'm talking about."

Denton felt heat sting his face and not from the sun, either. "Grace is a grown woman with a mind of her own," he responded tersely.

"In this case, I hope she uses it wisely."

With those choice words, the rancher turned and made his way back up the steps.

Denton merely shook his head and climbed in his vehicle. Yet he didn't start it. He was still somewhat dazed by the rancher's veiled warning. Talk about putting him in his place… He didn't think this kind of person existed anymore or that anyone cared that much about his fellow neighbor and friend.

He didn't remember this closeness growing up here, or maybe he just didn't recognize it for what it was—friends looking out for friends. Not bad, if you liked someone meddling in your business, which he didn't.

So what now?

He stared at the azure-blue sky and thought he'd never seen a more perfect day. How come the sky never looked like this in Dallas? And how come he never felt this relaxed, like he had finally stitched the seams of his frayed life back together for the first time since the crash? He'd begun to think that tragic event had messed with his mind permanently. But since he'd been here, his gut had uncoiled, and he'd actually laughed and smelled flowers, literally.

Ah, to hell with that kind of thinking. That would only get him in more trouble, mess with his mind in a different way. These country people were getting to him. He couldn't allow that. His goal was to get Grace out of here.

Himself as well.

So what was he waiting for? He'd gotten the deal that would elevate him to partner. But for some reason it no longer seemed that big a deal. Maybe it was because he had no legitimate reason for remaining in Ruby another minute.

Except Grace.

And he had no intention of leaving without her. After they had parted last evening, he'd gone to his room, taken a much-needed cold shower, then called

Ward's house and found that he had returned from the range and would see him first thing this morning.

Now he had to make a decision. He could forget her, forget how hot and pliant, how willing she was to please him in bed, how much he ached to be with her, *in* her. He could forget her smile that could and would explode into laughter at unexpected times, her lovely curves, her warm generosity...

Or he could plead with her again to go with him. He'd just have to use more patience, devote more time to her than he'd thought, plead his case more eloquently. That latter thought made him smile.

An attorney.

Amazing. Yet he couldn't figure out why he'd been so shocked. After all, Grace had all the right stuff to do anything she wanted. He just couldn't believe she'd chosen the field of law.

His smile spread. He would bet she'd been one tough litigator, waltzing into that courtroom looking like a delicate rose, only then to jab with hidden thorns anyone who crossed her.

Ouch!

Suddenly disgusted with those crazy thoughts and his blatant waste of time, Denton sped off toward the B&B. He was nearly there when he saw it. *Smoke.* It curled out of the kitchen window. The old home was on fire.

Grace! Oh, God! His heart almost stopped as he rammed down on the accelerator.

Eighteen

By the time he finally made it into the drive, Denton's legs were so heavy he didn't know if he could move them. But move them he did, fear for Grace's safety giving him the strength he needed to hurl himself out of the car and into the house.

"Grace!" he shouted at the top of his lungs. "Where are you?"

No answer.

His panic burgeoned as he dashed to the kitchen where the billows of smoke were pouring through the door. In the distance he heard the sound of fire engines. Without them, this old structure wouldn't have a chance to survive. If they didn't hurry, it wouldn't, anyway, he thought in desperation, taking the stairs three at a time.

"Grace!" he called again. Where the hell was she?

He dashed in and out of every room while all sorts

of terrible images colored his mind. The thought of her lying unconscious on the floor somewhere made him crazy. By the time he covered the entire house, his lungs had been stretched to the breaking point with both anxiety and smoke.

Coughing into his handkerchief, he finally dashed outside and sucked fresh air deep into his lungs. That was when he noticed her sitting on a stone bench under a huge oak, looking as lost and forlorn as a young child who had just buried her favorite pet.

Without saying a word, he closed the distance between them, reached for her and pulled her trembling body against his chest. She didn't protest.

"Are you all right?"

"I'm…fine."

"Are you sure?"

"I'm sure." She raised her head, her tear-stained eyes glistening.

"You scared the hell out me," he muttered, reaching out and trapping a tear with a finger.

"Again, I'm okay," she said, her voice shaky.

Still, he didn't stop running his hands over her. For his own peace of mind, he had to keep reassuring himself that she had indeed escaped injury.

"But my house isn't," she wailed suddenly, slumping against him and burying her head in his chest.

"Don't," he'd said brokenly, feeling so helpless, so damn useless.

He loved her.

That truth hit him with all the force of a sledgehammer upside his head. For a moment he reeled, the mental punch setting him back on his heels. In reality, he'd probably never stopped loving her. When push had come to shove, he'd been just too young and too pigheaded to know that.

"My…house…"

"Shh, it's okay. If the house goes, it can be rebuilt."

"That's easy for you to say," she'd sobbed.

"Hey, it will be easy. As long as you or anyone else didn't come to any harm, nothing else really matters."

"Thank God all the guests had gone and Connie wasn't working."

"What about you?"

"I had just come from the grocery store. I saw the smoke when I turned the corner and called the fire department from my cell phone."

"Your quick actions probably saved the house."

She didn't respond, just remained quiet in his arms until the fireman came after them, having assessed the damages and the cause, the fire having started from a faulty electrical switch in the kitchen. Once that had been taken care of, they made their way to the front porch. She couldn't seem to remain inside even though the smoke damage was not all that bad.

"I should be asking you if you're all right," she said out of the blue, facing him.

"Why?"

"You're so uptight."

"Dammit, Grace, I told you, you scared the hell out of me. Of course I'm uptight."

"I'm…sorry."

"I'm not leaving without you."

"I'm not going to Dallas," she said softly, meeting his intense gaze head-on.

"Then I'll stay here."

Her jaw dropped. "Why, you won't, either."

His cell phone chose that moment to ring. Cursing, he reached for it. "Dammit, Todd, I know it's important. Look, I'll call you back." With that he slammed his phone shut, and for a moment another silence fell between them.

"Your boss has spoken." He heard the bitterness in her tone and the resignation.

"I'm not going back, Grace."

She cut him an incredulous look. "And just why would you stay here?

"Because I love you, and you won't leave."

Her eyes widened and her lips parted. "You...love me?"

"Yes," he rasped, "and I want to marry you."

"Oh, Denton," she cried, flinging herself back in his arms, tears gushing down her cheeks. "I love you, too, you big oaf."

"So will you marry me?"

Laughter bled through her tears. "Just try and stop me."

She didn't think she would ever feel him inside her again. She was happy she'd been wrong. Yet she still couldn't believe that Denton loved her and wanted to marry her.

If he hadn't proved his love over and over with his hands, his lips, his tongue, his manhood, she still might not be convinced. But every place he touched, *every touch,* spoke of love and commitment. He seemed to worship her body as he made love to her over and over.

Even now, with the sunlight filtering though the sheers, he was continuing to love her.

His mouth was suckling a breast while a hand was cupping the warmth at the apex of her thighs, a finger sliding in and out of her wetness at will. She moaned under the sweet assault, snaking her hand down to him and surrounding his hardness.

He moaned, opening his eyes and staring into hers.

"Turnabout's fair play," she whispered, her eyes and voice soft and warm as honey.

"It's your time to be on top," he ground out, shifting her until their positions were reversed and he was hard and high inside her, her breasts full and throbbing under the tutelage of his hands.

"Oh, yes, darling," she cried, feeling him expand inside her.

He stared up at her through dazed eyes. "Tell me when."

"Now!"

It was then that she felt him explode, and she cried out in exquisite relief as she rode him harder and harder. His moans were the last thing she heard before lowering her cheek to his sweaty chest and feeling his arms close around her.

A short time later she peered up into his fervent gaze, then stretched.

He tapped at her lips, an indulgent smile on his face. "You look as satisfied as a cat."

"I am," she responded, grinning. "Hey, don't you think we should get up and get moving."

"Nope."

"In case you don't remember, buster, I had a fire here yesterday. I have things to do."

"And I guess you think I don't."

Suddenly Grace frowned, feeling her heart lurch. "As a matter of fact, what are you going to do?"

After he'd confessed his love and his intention to remain in Ruby, they hadn't talked about anything. Instead they had made love, which had been fine with her. But now, reality was staring them in the face, and they had to deal with it, though she was reluctant.

It still hadn't soaked in that Denton loved her and wanted to marry her. Even more mind-boggling was his intention to live in Ruby. That was why this conversation was so important.

"First things first, my darling," Denton said.

"I'm listening."

"When will you marry me?"

"As soon as you want."

"How about a large wedding?"

"No, absolutely not." Her tone was as emphatic as her words.

"Are you sure? I don't mind, though I'd rather not go through that long process."

"Not to worry, I don't, either. I just want our wedding to be small and cozy."

He kissed her. "Our wedding. I do love that thought."

"What about your parents?" She hated asking that loaded question, but she didn't have any choice. When she'd dated him years ago, Earl and Shirley Hardesty hadn't thought she was good enough for their son. She suspected they would feel the same way now. And while she wasn't marrying his parents, she knew it was important for Denton to have their approval. Hers, too, for that matter.

"What about them?"

"Don't do that. You know how they feel about me."

"Hell, that was years ago. You've changed.

They've changed. Mom's been riding my butt to marry again and give them some grandchildren.''

"Really?"

"Really."

For some reason she went short of breath. "And how do you feel about that?"

His eyes blazed into hers. "I hope we've already made a baby. Nothing would please me more than to watch your tummy swell with our child."

"Oh, Denton," she cried, pulling his head down and kissing him with ardent passion.

"If you have any more questions, then you'd better behave," he said in a strained voice. "I'm on a tight leash here, and you're running out of time."

She smiled, having felt his hardness once again poking in her lower stomach. "I still want an answer to my question. What makes you think you'll be happy here? I really can't ask you to give up your dream for mine, Denton. If so, you'll come to resent me."

"Hey, who said I'm giving up my dream?"

"You. This partnership in the company is what you want."

"It's what I thought I wanted. There's a difference."

"But—"

"No buts, my darling. What I really want is you and a plant nursery."

"Huh?"

"You heard me. I'm going to buy Flora out, if she'll let me."

Grace looked at him aghast. "Are you serious?"

"As serious as your fire."

"Oh, Denton, I don't know what to say."

"Say that you'll get up and fix me some breakfast."

"I can't," she wailed. "I don't have a kitchen."

"Then I guess I'll go get us something. Already having to wait on my wife."

She grinned, then winked. "Ain't it sweet?"

Nineteen

They were on the front porch a short time later, having just finished bagels, cream cheese and fruit. Now they were in the swing drinking the rest of the coffee.

"Not nearly as good as your chow-down grub, but it'll do in a crunch."

"Again it's a good thing all the guests are gone, though I have no idea how long I'll be out of commission."

"Not long. I'm going to find a contractor today."

Grace frowned. "That's not your responsibility."

"Hey, woman, let me take care of you, okay?"

She shrugged, a warm feeling replacing her concern. "Okay."

He grinned. "Man, you're easy."

She giggled, happier than she'd ever been in her life, though she knew there would be a lot of rough spots to get over. But if they truly loved each other, then they could make it.

"Denton—"

His cell phone rang. "Dammit," he muttered, grabbing it.

She turned her head and tried not to listen, but she couldn't stop herself. It was Todd, of course, and from the gist of the conversation he was livid. Her heart plummeted to her toes.

Even after he flipped his phone shut, the silence lingered.

"Don't go," she whispered.

"I have to. All hell's broken loose, and it's something I'm responsible for."

She lunged out of the swing and walked over to a post.

"Grace, it's okay," he said, coming up behind her but not touching her. "Actually, it's better than okay. While I'm there, I'll go ahead and wrap up things in the office, then I won't have to go back."

She swung around. "I don't want you to go at all."

"You know better than that, honey. I have an office, a home, lots to take care of."

"Do it later."

A deep frown doubled the wrinkles in his forehead. "I would, if it weren't for the crisis in the office."

"I still wish you'd wait," she said, feeling panic growing inside her, remembering the other time he left town and never came back.

"Hey, what's this really all about?" he asked, running the back of his hand down one side of her cheek.

"I'm afraid you'll get there and decide not to ever come back."

He released a sigh. "Like I did before?"

"Yes."

"I was a stupid boy then, Grace, who didn't have sense enough to get in out of a good, hard rain."

"Still—"

He gave her a hard, wet kiss. "That's not going to happen this time. I know where I want to be and with whom. Returning to Dallas is not going to change that."

"How can I be sure?"

"You can start by trusting me."

"Yeah, right."

His face turned red and his lips thinned. "Don't make this any harder than it is. Hell, I don't want to leave you, either." He paused, then snapped his fingers. "Why don't you come with me? That's the solution to this problem."

She really pushed the panic button then. "No way. I'm not leaving Ruby."

"God, Grace, you're hardheaded. Actually, that's the perfect solution, what with the house being out of commission and the repair work about to start."

"No," she said adamantly, her anxiety expanding.

"Dammit, what do you want me to do?"

"I told you. Don't go."

"I have to, and that's that."

She stiffened and stared at him for long moment. "If you walk down those steps and drive off, you need not bother to return."

He flinched visibly as though she'd slapped him in the face. Then his face darkened with suppressed anger. "You can't mean that?" he said harshly.

"Every word."

"But that's crazy! You're being both stubborn and irrational."

"I've told you how I feel."

"Well, I'm sorry, but I have no choice, and that's how I feel."

"Then I guess that's that."

He appeared ready to explode, but when he spoke, his voice was under control though it shook, "Again, if you don't trust me, then our love is doomed, anyway, so what the hell."

Refusing to let his tone and the devastated look on his face crack another hole in her heart, she turned her back.

He gave a strangled oath, then she heard him stalk down the stairs. Seconds later his vehicle was roaring down the drive. Somehow she managed to remain upright until she made it inside the house. Then she sank to the floor and sobbed.

"How much longer do you intend to go on like this?"

"Like how?" Grace asked innocently of Zelma, who was sitting at the bar sipping a cup of hot apple cider.

"Don't play the innocent with me, dear. It won't work."

"Oh, Zelma, I can't talk about it." Grace clamped down on her lower lip to keep it steady. "It hurts too much."

She knew she looked like hell, had ever since Denton left Ruby, which had been three weeks ago now. Although she cried herself to sleep every night, the days were tolerable, maybe because she'd been so busy. Despite their split, Denton had followed through with the promise of contacting a contractor, who had started working two days later. The man and his crew had been a lifesaver, getting the B&B back in operation on record time.

She had two of the guest rooms filled and the other one soon to be that way. Meanwhile Ed and Zelma had returned to Ruby and rented a house until they could build.

Grace couldn't imagine what she would've done without Zelma. She'd been both an emotional and physical rock, even though sometimes, like now, she made Grace crazy with her logic.

She didn't want to see herself as the heavy here— only Denton.

"So life goes on as is, huh?" Zelma was saying.

"And it's a good life, too," Grace said, still on the defensive.

"Sure." Zelma slid off the stool and peered around the kitchen. "I have to say this place actually looks better. I love the cream-colored paint you chose."

"Thanks. I'm pleased, too."

"I'm worried about you, Gracie. The spark's gone. It's a good thing the nuclear plant issue's been settled in our favor. You're definitely not up to that kind of fight."

"You're right, I'm not."

"Do you think Denton had anything to do with them choosing another site?"

"Maybe. He said he was going to use what influence he had. And the fact that he went through with contacting a contractor for the house leads me to believe he followed through with that, as well." She doubted he went through with purchasing the nursery from Flora, however. She hadn't had the courage to go there, much less pose such a question.

"What a man."

"Don't, Zelma."

"Okay, as long as you start working on getting yourself back together. I hate seeing you like this."

"I'm working on it," Grace said in as light a tone as she could.

Zelma was quiet for a while as if in deep thought, then she leaned over and hugged Grace. "He's right, you know. Love without trust isn't true love."

"Zelma!"

"I know I said I'd back off, but you're too damn stubborn for your own good. But then you know that."

"Maybe, but I have to do what I think is best."

"And you think being miserable and alone is best?"

Grace flushed. "You don't know all the details."

"I know what you've told me, and that's enough to know that you're wrong."

"Please, let's drop the subject, okay?"

"Whatever," Zelma said with a shrug, then stood. "I've got to run. I'll call you tomorrow."

Later that evening Grace climbed out of the shower and dressed in a casual pair of slacks and top. Once her makeup was done, she stared at herself in the mirror. All dressed up with no place to go.

Tears filled her eyes and she cursed silently. She missed Denton. The hole in her heart grew bigger every day. What did she expect? She played that awful evening over in her mind every time she closed her eyes, always with the same conclusion. Denton was right: if she couldn't trust him, she didn't love him.

But she did love him. More than life itself.

So what was her problem? Suddenly it hit her that

she didn't have a problem other than her pride, which seemed to lose its importance now. Her breathing quickened. Was it too late to repair the damages? But to do so, she'd have to leave Ruby and go to Dallas.

She grabbed her chest and visibly staggered backward. Could she do that? Could she leave her safety net and take a chance and go for the gold?

Without the net?

Sweat dotted her skin, and her breathing turned more rapid. No, she wouldn't have a panic attack. She would ignore her elevated breathing and her rapid pulse and take action by doing what she should've done days, weeks, ago.

By damn, she was going to the city. To Denton.

"Hell, Hardesty, I'm so sick of you moping around here like a lovesick puppy, I could puke."

"Thanks, Todd, and you can go to hell."

"I have a better suggestion. Why don't you go get laid. Maybe that'll take the edge off."

"Not interested."

Todd rubbed the back of his neck, then stared back at Denton out of bleak eyes. They were in Todd's office discussing a client who had given them trouble and whom they were considering dropping. It was a touchy matter that required Denton's full concentration, an asset that was hard to come by.

He moaned inwardly. He couldn't think about her, talk about her, dream about her without coming apart at the seams. Todd, more than anyone else, knew this. But he was getting tired of it, too, and Denton couldn't blame him. He had to either come to terms with his loss or change the terms.

"I wish the hell you were interested in something," Todd muttered under his breath.

"I am. Grace."

"Then why aren't you there with her, for God's sake? I want you to do what will make you happy, and Lord knows, you're one miserable sonofabitch."

Suddenly Denton stood. "You're right. I am going to do something about that. I love her too much to let her off the hook that easily.

"It's about time you started thinking with your brain instead of below the waist."

For the first time in a long while, Denton grinned. "Good advice."

Several hours later he mounted the steps of the B&B with his heart in his throat. He nearly choked on it when Grace chose that moment to open the door, her purse and keys in hand.

"Oh," she whimpered, pulling up short and staring up at him, shocked.

He swallowed forcefully. "Uh, hi."

"Hi."

Silence.

He swallowed again. "Were you going somewhere?" he asked inanely, drinking in her beauty, her smell, aching to touch her, taste her.

"To Dallas," she whispered, "to see you, to ask you to forgive me."

It took what seemed like eons for her words to soak in, but when they did, he cried with joy and at the same time he grabbed her and buried his face in her hair.

"Oh, Grace, I love you, and I'm sorry, too."

She pulled back, love shining from her eyes. "You

have nothing to be sorry for. You just loved me, and I couldn't see that.''

''Let's get married.''

''Now?''

''Now.''

She laughed. ''Let's do it!''

With a loud shout he swung her up in his arms and carried her down the steps. ''Oh, by the way, I bought the nursery.''

''Fantastic!''

He paused and stared down into her adoring, up-turned face. ''Know that you're loved from the depths of my being,'' he whispered before lowering his head.

She clung to him as her greedy lips collided with his.

*   *   *   *   *

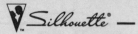

SILHOUETTE®
MAKES YOU
A STAR!

Feel like a star with Silhouette.

We will fly you and a guest to New York City for an
exciting weekend stay at a glamorous 5-star hotel.
Experience a refreshing day at one of New York's
trendiest spas and have your photo taken by a
professional. Plus, receive $1,000 U.S. spending money!

**Flowers...long walks...dinner for two...
how does Silhouette Books
make romance come alive for you?**

Send us a script, with 500 words or less, along with visuals (only drawings,
magazine cutouts or photographs or combination thereof). Show us how
Silhouette Makes Your Love Come Alive. Be creative and have fun. No
purchase necessary. All entries must be clearly marked with your name,
address and telephone number. All entries will become property of
Silhouette and are not returnable. **Contest closes September 28, 2001.**

Please send your entry to: **Silhouette Makes You a Star!**

In U.S.A.	In Canada
P.O. Box 9069	P.O. Box 637
Buffalo, NY, 14269-9069	Fort Erie, ON, L2A 5X3

Look for contest details on the next page, by visiting www.eHarlequin.com or
request a copy by sending a self-addressed envelope to the applicable address
above. Contest open to Canadian and U.S. residents who are 18 or over.
Void where prohibited.

Silhouette®
Where love comes alive™

Our lucky winner's photo will appear in a Silhouette ad. Join the fun!

SRMYAS1

HARLEQUIN "SILHOUETTE MAKES YOU A STAR!" CONTEST 1308
OFFICIAL RULES
NO PURCHASE NECESSARY TO ENTER

1. To enter, follow directions published in the offer to which you are responding. Contest begins June 1, 2001, and ends on September 28, 2001. Entries must be postmarked by September 28, 2001, and received by October 5, 2001. Enter by hand-printing (or typing) on an 8 ½" x 11" piece of paper your name, address (including zip code), contest number/name and attaching a script containing <u>500 words or less, along with drawings, photographs or magazine cutouts, or combinations thereof</u> (i.e., collage) <u>on no larger than 9" x 12"</u> piece of paper, describing how the <u>Silhouette books make romance come alive for you.</u> Mail via first-class mail to: Harlequin "Silhouette Makes You a Star!" Contest 1308, (in the U.S.) P.O. Box 9069, Buffalo, NY 14269-9069, (in Canada) P.O. Box 637, Fort Erie, Ontario, Canada L2A 5X3. Limit one entry per person, household or organization.

2. Contests will be judged by a panel of members of the Harlequin editorial, marketing and public relations staff. Fifty percent of criteria will be judged against script and fifty percent will be judged against drawing, photographs and/or magazine cutouts. Judging criteria will be based on the following:

   - Sincerity—25%
   - Originality and Creativity—50%
   - Emotionally Compelling—25%

   In the event of a tie, duplicate prizes will be awarded. Decisions of the judges are final.

3. All entries become the property of Torstar Corp. and may be used for future promotional purposes. Entries will not be returned. No responsibility is assumed for lost, late, illegible, incomplete, inaccurate, nondelivered or misdirected mail.

4. Contest open only to residents of the U.S. <u>(except Puerto Rico)</u> and Canada who are 18 years of age or older, and is void wherever prohibited by law; all applicable laws and regulations apply. Any litigation within the Province of Quebec respecting the conduct or organization of a publicity contest may be submitted to the Régie des alcools, des courses et des jeux for a ruling. Any litigation respecting the awarding of a prize may be submitted to the Régie des alcools, des courses et des jeux only for the purpose of helping the parties reach a settlement. Employees and immediate family members of Torstar Corp. and D. L. Blair, Inc., their affiliates, subsidiaries and all other agencies, entities and persons connected with the use, marketing or conduct of this contest are not eligible to enter. Taxes on prizes are the sole responsibility of the winner. Acceptance of any prize offered constitutes permission to use winner's name, photograph or other likeness for the purposes of advertising, trade and promotion on behalf of Torstar Corp., its affiliates and subsidiaries without further compensation to the winner, unless prohibited by law.

5. Winner will be determined no later than November 30, 2001, and will be notified by mail. Winner will be required to sign and return an Affidavit of Eligibility/Release of Liability/Publicity Release form within 15 days after winner notification. Noncompliance within that time period may result in disqualification and an alternative winner may be selected. All travelers must execute a Release of Liability prior to ticketing and must possess required travel documents (e.g., passport, photo ID) where applicable. Trip must be booked by December 31, 2001, and completed within one year of notification. No substitution of prize permitted by winner. Torstar Corp. and D. L. Blair, Inc., their parents, affiliates and subsidiaries are not responsible for errors in printing of contest, entries and/or game pieces. In the event of printing or other errors that may result in unintended prize values or duplication of prizes, all affected game pieces or entries shall be null and void. **Purchase or acceptance of a product offer does not improve your chances of winning.**

6. Prizes: (1) Grand Prize—A 2-night/3-day trip for two (2) to New York City, including round-trip coach air transportation nearest winner's home and hotel accommodations (double occupancy) at The Plaza Hotel, a glamorous afternoon makeover at <u>a trendy New York spa,</u> $1,000 in U.S. spending money and an opportunity to <u>have a professional photo taken and appear in a Silhouette advertisement</u> (approximate retail value: $7,000). (10) Ten Runner-Up Prizes of gift packages (retail value $50 ea.). Prizes consist of only those items listed as part of the prize. Limit one prize per person. Prize is valued in U.S. currency.

7. For the name of the winner (available after December 31, 2001) send a self-addressed, stamped envelope to: Harlequin "Silhouette Makes You a Star!" Contest 1197 Winners, P.O. Box 4200 Blair, NE 68009-4200 or you may access the www.eHarlequin.com Web site through February 28, 2002.

Contest sponsored by Torstar Corp., P.O Box 9042, Buffalo, NY 14269-9042.

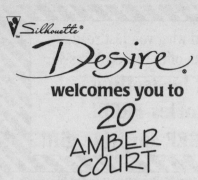

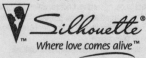